DASHING

KYLIE GILMORE

Dashing: © 2021 by Kylie Gilmore

Cover design by: Michele Catalano Creative

Published by: Extra Fancy Books

ISBN-13: 978-1-64658-023-1

Can men and women be friends? Maybe.

1

Adam

"Would you like to dance?" a cheerful voice asks, and an alarm goes off in my mind.

I should've anticipated this, a slow song at our siblings' wedding reception. I meet the bright and eager brown eyes of my only woman friend ever, Kayla Winters.

She's a goddess, no question, wearing a sleeveless black dress for the occasion, exposing creamy skin from her delicate throat to her collarbones and the swell of her cleavage. Her dark brown hair falls in a wave over one bare shoulder. Her plump lips are a luscious red. I swallow hard.

Ridiculous. We're friends. No cause for alarm. Of course I can slow dance with my woman friend. Neither of us is interested in a relationship. She specifically said she wasn't ready to even consider dating after getting left at the altar. It's one of the first things she told me, and she continues to stick by her firm stance, as she'll share with anyone who suggests she get back out there. As for me, just the *idea* of a committed relationship sets me on edge.

I take her hand and walk out to the dance floor. It occurs to me she only dated her ex-fiancé for two months, while Kayla and I have known each other for four months now. Since last February when she decided we were friends.

She actually said that back then. *You seem like a really nice guy, and I'd like to be friends.* What could I say? She's my client's younger sister, and I was on the job for weeks. I'm a master carpenter. Of course I agreed, even though I never have women friends. Truthfully, I've always been a bit of a lone wolf. My work, my family, the people I know in town, that's enough for me. I guess you could say I'm friends with the guy next door I sometimes go fishing with, but it's not like we share deep confidences. Kayla did right from the beginning. My quiet nature seems to make her comfortable enough to share.

I find us an open spot on the dance floor and bring my hands to her narrow waist, holding her lightly. She puts her arms around my neck instead of holding my shoulders, bringing us so close I can feel her heat. Or maybe that's my heat. I'm burning up in my dress shirt, the blazer discarded long ago. She's petite, even in heels, her head level with my chest.

I subtly shift her away from me. It seems more appropriate for friends. Even if she was over her sleazeball ex, I'd never cross the line. It's important to keep that boundary so no one gets hurt.

"It's a beautiful wedding, isn't it?" she asks, looking around us. We're under a white tent in the groom's backyard, an expansive piece of land with rolling hills edged by woodlands. My younger sister, Sydney, married Kayla's older brother, Wyatt. I guess Kayla and I are related now. Some kind of in-law thing. That's cool since we're good friends.

I glance around. "Yeah. And they lucked out getting a sunny day." It's May, typically sunny. I'm barely aware of what I'm saying I'm so focused on keeping a safe distance. She keeps shifting closer.

"I ordered it special," she declares. "You know, if I weren't going to be a biostatistician, I think I'd make a good wedding planner. I helped Sydney plan this one."

I incline my head. I don't know anything about either career. All I know is she's whip smart and just wrapped up her master's degree in biostatistics. She'll be looking for a job soon, probably moving far away from Summerdale, New York. Right now she works part time as a waitress at The Horseman Inn, the historic restaurant and bar that's been in my family for generations. My sister, Sydney, owns it now. Kayla is a terrible waitress, constantly dropping dishes, but she's so damn cute and apologetic everyone forgives her.

She smiles. "You look very handsome in your crisp white dress shirt. Nice contrast with your dark hair and tanned skin. Still got the scruffy jaw. No shaving for the wedding, huh?"

She never talks about my looks, always my skill as a craftsman. I'm suddenly hyperaware of her, of me, every nerve ending on edge. "Uh, thanks. I trimmed the scruff a bit to make it look neat."

"Mmm-hmm. Got a haircut too."

I go stock-still at the surprising sensation of her fingers running through the hair at the nape of my neck, sending tingles down my spine. *She's playing with my hair.* Even more alarming, she goes up on tiptoe to whisper in my ear, her full breasts grazing my chest. "We're friends, right?"

"Yeah." I relax a little. Both because she's keeping the boundary and because she shifted back to look at me, ensuring her breasts are now a safe distance away.

She smiles winningly. "Great. I have a favor to ask you."

"Sure."

She laughs. "You didn't even hear what it is. What if I said something crazy like I need you to do my laundry?"

A smile tugs at my lips. "If you don't mind wrinkled clothes, I'll throw them in with mine."

She smooths a hand down my shirtsleeve, sending a rush of heat over my skin. "Your clothes aren't wrinkled at all."

"I pull dress shirts out of the dryer immediately to avoid ironing. What do you need?"

She looks over my shoulder, suddenly shy. "You're going to think it's silly."

I don't reply. Kayla never needs any coaxing to talk.

She goes back on tiptoe to whisper her request, and I catch

the pink of her cheek out of the corner of my eye. "Would you pretend to be my fiancé at a party?"

I break into a cold sweat. *Fiancé?* I was a fiancé once, never again.

"I'll pay you," she adds.

My jaw gapes.

She grabs my hand and tugs me off the dance floor, saying, "I'll explain in private."

"No need to explain." *Because it's not happening.* No payment and definitely no fiancé, pretend or not.

She releases my hand and gestures for me to follow as she walks around to the front of Wyatt's large gray two-story house. I don't mind getting away from the reception with so many people. I like the quiet. She climbs the steps of the wraparound porch with four white pine rocking chairs. I made those chairs, a simple elegant design with curved wood to fit your head and bottom. They were additional pieces Wyatt commissioned me to do, along with a library complete with shelves, storage space, and a rolling ladder. I restored some hardwood floors and did cabinetry in the living room too. He's been good for my business, talking me up and giving me loads of referrals.

She sits in a chair and rocks a little. "I just love these chairs, you crafty genius."

My chest puffs with pride. I take the chair next to her. "Thanks." I work hard at my craft, and I'm always trying to improve, taking on more challenges.

She gives me a sheepish smile. "So, it's like this. My favorite professor is having an end-of-the-year party at her place for the entire statistics department. It's casual, a back-yard barbecue. And my ex—the one who left me at the altar four and a half months ago—will be there. This is the first time I'm going to see him since then, and I know it'll be awkward. I just want him to see I've moved on *definitively*."

She's very precise when it comes to numbers—four and *a half* months. I respect that as a carpenter. You have to measure twice before you cut anything. Now that I know it's about saving face in front of her sleazy ex, I'm in. I'm about to tell her that when she continues.

"I know it's an inconvenience for you, which is why I'm happy to pay you. My tips aren't great, honestly, but my apartment is free, so I do have some money."

She lives above The Horseman Inn in my sister's old place. Not surprising her tips aren't great when she dumps food on patrons and the floor. I let that one go. "First, please don't pay a guy for a date."

"But it's an inconvenience."

I exhale sharply. "Second, I'll go."

She blinks a few times. "You will?"

"Yeah."

"And you don't want anything in return?"

I rub the back of my neck, not expecting to have to explain the way friendship works. Will it be uncomfortable? Yes. But I want to be there for her. "I got your back."

She stares at me, not seeming convinced. "I don't know. Now that I think about it, you don't like parties. This wouldn't be fun for you at all. Forget it. It wasn't fair of me to ask. I'll ask someone else, okay?"

Before I can reply, she's already walking away, on her way to her new fake fiancé.

I stare after her, torn on what to do. Do I insist on being her fake fiancé? It's true I don't enjoy parties, but she asked me for a reason, right? I'm the friend she can depend on. Maybe I didn't sound enthusiastic enough.

I follow her around the side of the house. Her sisters, Brooke and Paige, wave at her from the dance floor, and she hurries over to them, joining in with enthusiastic hip bumps for her sisters. Kinda funny because she's shorter than they are.

Someone jabs me in the ribs. I turn, coming face-to-face with Kayla's brother, Wyatt. My new brother-in-law is my age, thirty, and about my height at six feet with dark brown wavy hair, brown eyes, and a neatly trimmed beard. He's good to my sister and quick with a joke. Though right now he looks damn serious.

"Hey, congrats, man," I say.

"What was that about?" he asks, jutting his chin toward Kayla. She's the youngest of his three sisters, and he looks out for them fiercely. Probably something to do with the fact that their dad died when they were young and Wyatt stepped up. Kayla went straight to him when she was left at the altar and stuck around too.

I pull my shoulders back, immediately sensing overprotective brother about to go on the attack. "Nothing." I'm not going to share Kayla's fake-fiancé plan with her brother. That's a betrayal of trust.

"Look, I could tell she was propositioning you on the dance floor—"

"Say what?"

He holds up a palm. "Save it. It's not that I don't like you, I do, and I respect your work, but—" he jabs a finger in my chest "—don't mess around with her unless you're serious. I'm talking marriage level of commitment because that's what she's looking for."

A chill goes through me. *Never again.*

"It's not like that," I say. "We're friends."

He scoffs. "I saw how cozy you looked together on the dance floor. It might've started off like that when she talked your ear off while you worked at my house, but I've seen you at The Horseman Inn while she's working, and you look damn happy." Wyatt sometimes works behind the bar there. Not because he has to—he's a retired billionaire tech whiz— but because he's passionate about quality wine, beer, and whiskey and wants to share that knowledge with customers. Sydney says profits at the bar are way up as a result.

I lift one shoulder in a careless shrug. He's got no bone to pick with me. I'm not getting involved with his sister. Period. "It's my family's restaurant. I always go there."

He grunts. "She's not a woman you mess around with. Got it?"

"Loud and clear."

He turns to me with a speculative eye. "Unless you're serious."

I put my palms up. "I've got no plans to marry her." I was engaged a little over a year ago. Amelia left for an "adventure in Panama" with a consultant from her work. After four years together, it was a shock. Understatement. My dad died a week later. I've only recently started to feel like myself again.

He shakes his head. "After her asshole ex bailed on their wedding, she was a complete mess for two months. You didn't see half of what I saw. Brutal."

"It's been four and a half months."

He eyes me.

"Just saying."

He slices a hand through the air. "Doesn't matter. Be serious or forget it. Those are your two options."

This is my new brother-in-law, whom I consider a friend. He gave me a dream job with free rein to design his library and living room built-ins, plus I'm getting steady work referrals through him. It's amazing how many wealthy people he knows who appreciate custom carpentry work. I'm not going to screw that up.

I clap a hand on his shoulder. "Kayla and I are friends. End of story."

We both look over to Kayla on the dance floor. She's balancing on one foot, working off one strappy heel. She loses her balance, and Wyatt and I both lurch forward. Sydney rights her before either of us can get close.

Wyatt gives me a suspicious look before joining Sydney on the dance floor.

I head for the open bar, get a whisky—Wyatt stocked the good stuff—and take a seat at an empty table. My eye catches on Kayla. Now she's dancing with my brother Eli. He's closer to her age at twenty-six, thick with muscle because he works out hard-core to keep in shape for his job as a cop. Not that he has to apprehend any criminals in Summerdale. We're pretty low-key here.

Wait. Is she asking him to be her fake fiancé? He's single and won't hesitate to make a move. I'm on my feet before I know what I'm doing. "Kayla."

She turns to me. "Hey, Adam! Join us!" She waves me over.

Eli says something to her, and she pushes his shoulder playfully. He's probably telling her I never cut loose. I've never been a big partier. And you won't find me having an "adventure in Panama" either. I'm rooted here in Summerdale with my job and my family, but that doesn't mean I don't have fun in my own way.

And then she's heading straight for me, and my pulse thrums through my veins.

She looks up at me, a quizzical look on her sweet face. "What's up?"

"Is Eli going to that party with you?"

She glances back at him. "I don't know. You think he'd do it?"

Of course he'd do it. He's all about making a move on a beautiful woman.

She starts moving to the beat. "We are friendly. I see him at the restaurant regularly. He's the Saturday night entertainment on his acoustic guitar sometimes."

Yes, the multitalented Eli. He only learned guitar to impress women.

She stills. "Are you okay? You look kinda mad."

I dip my head toward her ear and lower my voice. "I'll go with you to the party. I'm looking forward to sticking it to your ex."

Her eyes light up. "Really?" She throws her arms around my neck and kisses my cheek. Warmth rushes through me. "Thank you! I swear I'll return the favor somehow."

I let out a breath, relieved I don't have to think about Eli touching her. Not that I'm going to make a move. I'm her revenge date. *Fiancé*. Sweat runs down my spine.

This is all pretend. No commitment necessary.

Wyatt calls out to her.

She holds up a finger for him to wait and beams at me, her plump pouty lips spreading wide. She can't help having pouty lips. "Thanks again for *you know what*. We'll keep it a secret between us." She winks with a dazzling smile.

My gut tightens, the blood rushing through my veins. I ignore the inconvenient lust. Obviously, it's been too long for me. I care too much about her to get involved, ultimately hurting her because I can't give her what she wants, a serious relationship. And Wyatt warned me off for just that reason. Don't mess with his sister, with the implications being—family tension, losing all the work referrals he sends my way. It's personal and professional suicide. I'm not screwing things up with him.

I'm just doing her a favor so she can save face in front of her ex. That's all. It's a friend thing.

2

Kayla

Here I am with my fake fiancé, la la la. *Take that, Rob, you weasel!* Adam looks good too. Well, he always looks good—tall, lean with muscle, short brown hair with a scruffy jaw—but he looks *especially* good today. His white T-shirt shows off his tan, along with the cut of his biceps and corded muscular forearms. This is not a man who sits behind a computer all day. He works those muscles. His faded jeans fit his form deliciously. I'm sure any woman would agree his ass looks fine in those jeans. I've spent a decent amount of time admiring his muscular body from the back. Mostly because when I talked to him at Wyatt's house, Adam would be busy working while I stood behind him, chatting him up. That's how we became friends.

Just because I admire his booty doesn't mean I'm crossing the line. I'm not ready for a relationship after getting jilted at the altar. But I feel good when I'm around him, all warm and glowy. Adam is the kind of guy who keeps his word. When he said he'd be at Wyatt's house at eight a.m. the next day for work, he always showed up right on time. And today he picked me up exactly when he said he would. It means something when a person keeps their word.

"You doing okay?" he asks me for the third time.

We've been here for an hour and already made the rounds, talking to everyone. Rob's not here yet. I can't leave until he sees me with Adam.

I nod. "Are you okay?"

"Course. Don't worry about me."

I know parties aren't his scene. He's quiet and reserved, content to be with a small gathering or alone, but he warmed up with me right away. I like to think it's my friendly personality, but it was most likely sympathy for my devastated state post-altar dumping. At the time I felt compelled to share my woes. Rob and I dated two months, where he showered me with compliments, flowers, cards with mushy stuff written inside, the works. He proposed at our favorite restaurant, eager to make it official. We planned to elope at that very same restaurant on New Year's Eve. And then he got cold feet at the last minute while I stood there waiting in my beautiful wedding gown. Or so he said. I suspect the only reason he proposed was because I told him I was saving myself for marriage. *Weasel!*

"Not too much longer," I tell Adam.

He glances at my empty red plastic cup. "You want more wine?"

He's very attentive as a fake fiancé, which I appreciate. "Could you get me a bottled water instead?"

He takes my cup and walks off. A man of action and few words.

I glance around, looking for Rob. Not here yet. I can't wait around forever. This is an imposition on Adam, and he doesn't like to leave his English bulldog, Tank, alone too long either. Sometimes he has a neighbor go in and check on Tank if he has to be away for work out of town. Maybe that's how I can return the enormous favor he's doing for me today. I'll check in on Tank and give him cuddle time. I'll mention it on the way home.

Adam returns and hands me a bottled water.

"Thanks."

He jerks his chin at me. That's Adam for *you're welcome, no problem*. I'm good at filling in the blanks where Adam's concerned. For example, he hasn't mentioned I look nice in my outfit—light yellow blouse with a matching fluffy mini skirt—but he swallowed audibly when his gaze trailed down my bare legs. That's Adam for *great outfit to make your ex jealous, but I'm too polite as your guy friend to mention it.*

"Let's get something to eat," I say, heading for the long table of food. We help ourselves to burgers. I add potato salad to my plate, and Adam goes for the potato chips.

We eat standing together near the end of the table in companionable silence. I'm so annoyed that Rob is late, but what did I expect? He's always late, and you can't trust him to keep his commitments. Obviously, since he rushed me into an elopement, only to leave a message—not with me but with the restaurant owner—that he wouldn't be going through with it. It was his idea!

I take a ferocious bite of potato salad. At least Adam has been wonderful as my trusty companion here today. And it's easy to brag about him to everyone. He's a true craftsman, and you don't see work like his every day. He can do interesting modern designs for tables and end pieces with splayed legs, classic designs with intricately scrolled trim, and build just about any kind of furniture you can imagine, along with cabinetry and built-ins. He can even restore historic oak plank flooring so you can't tell it was ever touched. I've been showing off his online portfolio to everyone.

Only problem is, Adam's terrible at acting like we're a couple. He hasn't touched me at all. I should've given him some instructions. I bet he's new at the fake-fiancé thing. So am I, but at least I know we should be holding hands and/or putting an arm casually around each other. So far, I had to grab his hand every time I introduced him to someone.

Once we finish our dinner, Adam walks off with our paper plates to toss them in the garbage, leaving me alone just as Rob approaches. Crap. I can't run to Adam or it'll look like I'm avoiding Rob. I need to play it cool. Look at Rob wearing an *Always Summer* T-shirt from the online role-playing game where we met. After meeting online, we discovered we went to the same university. He's getting a PhD in statistics. Clueless man reminding me of our history with that shirt. Does he think we'll pick up where we left off? No way in hell.

I gesture to Adam to join me in what I hope is a nonfrantic way. He speeds up, sensing I need him. Finally, Adam reaches me a second before Rob.

Rob halts, looking surprised to see me with Adam. I can't let there be any question about Adam's relationship to me. I subtly take his hand and hold it behind my back so it looks like his arm is around me. I'm even wearing my sister Paige's old engagement ring for authenticity, a round diamond on a gold band. Her ex left for work overseas after they broke up, so she just put the ring in a drawer, figuring she'd pawn it one day. Luckily for me, it was still available.

I had a week to prepare for this event, and now that it's finally here, my heart is jackrabbiting against my rib cage. My ex looks the same as I remember—brown hair neatly parted to the side, pasty white skin, no muscle tone anywhere. I can't help but notice the contrast to the man I'm forcing to put an arm around me. Honestly, Rob is the brainy type I've always been drawn to.

"Hello," I say.

"Hi, Kayla," Rob says. "Long time no see."

Gee, I wonder why. Weasel!

"Yes," I say tightly. "It's been a while since you never showed up at our wedding. Fortunately, I've moved on." I gaze adoringly up at Adam.

Rob holds his hand out to Adam. "Hi, I'm Rob."

Adam ignores his hand. "I guess I should thank you for not following through with Kayla. Otherwise, we never would've connected."

I beam. "We're engaged." I hold up my ring hand.

"That was quick," Rob says, eying Adam speculatively. "I guess she told you her rule."

My cheeks flame. He's talking about my no-sex-until-marriage rule to imply Adam only wants me for *that*. *Double slime rat weasel!*

Adam turns to me, a question in his brown eyes. Mortification sets in, and then it gets worse.

Rob continues in a confidential tone to Adam. "Hope it's the real deal. Don't be like me, man. No hookup is worth being chained for life."

I suck in air. I suspected my V-card was the whole reason Rob rushed me to the altar, but to hear him say it out loud, and in front of Adam, is so much worse.

"What the hell are you talking about?" Adam barks at Rob.

Conversation quiets, and people gather closer.

My pulse races, every muscle tensing. "I'll explain later," I say to Adam under my breath.

Rob shrugs. "That's the whole reason I proposed. I got tired of waiting for her to give it up."

Adam moves fast, grabbing Rob by the shirt collar and hauling him up close. "Apologize to her. Now."

Rob pales, his eyes rolling toward me. "I'm sorry! I was just being honest."

Adam shoves him away. "Not good enough. A real apology."

"I only did the logical thing," Rob whines.

Adam draws back a fist, but I grab his arm, whispering, "Please don't make a scene." I can't even bear to look at the quiet witnesses around us.

He turns back to Rob. "You never talk to her. You don't even *look* at her again. Now get out of here before I kick your ass."

Rob hesitates, looking around him for backup. Adam charges forward, and Rob jumps, turns tail, and runs straight out of the yard to the street.

Conversation resumes in quiet murmurs.

I turn to Adam, his jaw tight, hands still in fists. I never knew he could be so protective. He's like a real-life knight in shining armor. Warmth steals through me.

I nudge his arm with my shoulder. "Thank you."

His eyes meet mine, his voice fierce. "He's so far beneath you. I hate that you were with someone like that."

A rush of affection has me giving him a sideways hug. His arm settles around my shoulders. Despite the fact I just experienced the second most humiliating moment of my life (the first being left at the altar), I feel almost giddy. Adam came through for me in the most amazing way.

I look up at him. "You're awesome."

"You okay?" he asks, still looking pissed off.

"Yeah, I'm good."

"You want to get out of here?"

"In a bit. I don't want it to be obvious I'm leaving because of him. Let's have a drink and mingle."

"Water?"

"Yes, please."

He walks over to the cooler by the patio for two more bottled waters. I glance around for the first time, but it seems everyone's gone back to normal conversation now that the possibility of a fistfight is gone.

I can't believe I was so blissfully ignorant of Rob's true intentions back when we were together. I truly thought he loved me. What if every guy sees me that way? I'll be thinking it's the real deal, they'll propose, and then they'll dump me at the last possible moment, not really wanting marriage so much as sex. My virginity was never meant to be bait.

Adam walks toward me with his relaxed easy stride. My stomach flutters unexpectedly, and I find myself smiling.

He hands me a bottled water. "What're you smiling about? I thought you'd be upset."

"My upset is countered by having a great friend like you."

He studies me for a moment, searching my expression. Whatever he sees there must put him at ease because he opens his water and takes a long drink. My gaze is drawn to his Adam's apple as it moves up and down his manly throat, and then to the cord of his neck, and up to the dark scruff on his square jaw. My breath quickens at his sexy good looks. Of course I always knew he was handsome, but this is somehow different. Every nerve ending tingles in awareness.

He leans down to my ear, his voice a deep rumble that sends a delicious shiver through me. "Think people bought the engagement?"

Our gazes collide up close, the air buzzing between us.

My mouth goes dry. "Yeah," I croak.

He inclines his head. "Good."

"Yeah, good," I echo.

Two women from my master's degree program walk over to chat, Julia and Yvette, exclaiming over my engagement ring and peppering me with questions about the proposal and how long we've been dating. They're both brunettes, single and down-to-earth like me. It's easy enough to talk about how Adam and I met while he was on the job at my brother's house. I brag about his great skill as a carpenter, showing off his work online while I scramble to think up a good proposal story.

"You're very talented," Julia says to Adam. "So how did you propose? Was it a big romantic gesture?"

"So romantic," I answer for him.

Adam nods but doesn't add to the story.

I jump in with the part I'd really like in my ideal proposal scenario. "He went down on one knee and just spoke from the heart. It was *everything*."

Julia and Yvette exchange a pleased look and turn back to me, smiling.

"So brave of you after *you-know-who*," Yvette whispers. "I never liked him."

"Opening your heart is always an act of bravery," I say. "How else can you let love in?" I turn to Adam for his agreement, but his expression is shuttered closed. Guess he's not comfortable with love talk in front of other people, even if it is pretend. I turn back to my friends. "I'm with the right person now, and that makes all the difference."

Talk quickly moves to what's on all of our minds now that we've finished our master's degrees in biostatistics—the job search. Adam stands by, listening quietly. When I finish my water, he takes my empty bottle to recycle without a word.

The moment he walks away, Julia says in an exaggerated upper-class tone, "He's quite dashing."

Yvette nods.

I smile. "He is." I sound a little dreamy. Well, that's okay, I'm supposed to be engaged to him.

As soon as Adam returns to my side, my friends hug me and say goodbye. They're heading back to the city after this. I'm ready to go now too.

"You have to get back to Tank," I tell Adam. "I'm just going to say goodbye to Professor Kurtz, and we'll be on our way."

"Sure."

I make my way through the mingling people in search of Professor Kurtz. I did what I came here to do, but there's one thing that's gnawing at me. Rob admitting he proposed just to get in my pants was a lightbulb moment. I need to deal with the giant pink V stamped on my forehead (or is it stamped somewhere lower?). Either way, taking Mom's advice to heart to wait for marriage was a giant mistake that will only get more difficult to explain to guys the older I get.

I'm twenty-five, for crying out loud! This is getting embarrassing. Is it my fault I've never met a man who tempted me enough to break my rule? Not even Rob. And what does that say about me that I was willing to marry a man I felt warmly toward but not passionate about? Truth is, of all the guys I've dated over the years, several were legit good kissers, but I never once felt carried away enough to cross the line. Is it possible I dated guys I wasn't super attracted to as an easy way to stick to my rule?

A real and disturbing possibility.

Clearly, I'm missing some vital knowledge for unlocking passion. Or maybe it's that I never trusted a guy to go below the waistline and stop if I needed him to. Maybe passion is only unlocked under the belly button. Huh.

I glance up at Adam, and a jolt of a new kind of awareness goes through me. Primal man-woman potential. Excitement with a chaser of nerves runs through my body, making me feel alive and aware and…sexual. He's handsome, kind, a protective sort. I feel safe with him. Hmm…

I spot Professor Kurtz and thank her for the party, giving her a hug goodbye. She's a brilliant woman in her forties with blond hair and glasses. She makes full-time academia and being a mom to two daughters look easy.

"Kayla, it's been a pleasure. I'm going to email you a contact I have at Noon Pharmaceuticals in Indiana. Maybe they'll have something that's right for you." She knows I'm on the job hunt.

"Thank you. I really appreciate it."

"Of course. And put me down for a reference everywhere you apply." She holds out a hand to Adam. "Nice to meet you, Adam. Hopefully I'll get an invite to your wedding. Kayla's special to me. A brilliant and curious mind."

Aww. "Definitely," I say.

Adam shakes her hand and grumbles something unintelligible. He's new at this.

I grab his hand, giving it a squeeze, and then we walk back to the street, where Adam parked his black Mazda.

The moment we're back in his car, I let out a breath of relief. "Mission accomplished. And even though Rob was a total ass, it only makes it easier for me to move on. Obviously, he's not worth another moment's thought."

"I still wish I could've gotten one good punch in."

I meet his fierce gaze, my protector. "What you did was plenty. I left the party with my head held high, and all people will remember was that Rob was an ass who ran off with his tail between his legs."

He turns on the car, blasts the air conditioner, and drives off at a nice slow acceleration. He's got such a patient quiet way about him. I bet he'd be patient with my inexperience too. A teacher of sorts, unlocking what I've been missing out on—passion. Just the idea of his big muscular body pressing against mine makes my breath quicken, my pulse race, and my entire body flush with heat. I'm onto something here. When we danced at Wyatt's wedding last week, there was definitely heat between us. Potential for more in a casual way? I know I'm not ready to seriously date, and when we first met and I spilled my woes to him, Adam commented that my devastation is the exact reason he avoids relationships. This could be perfect.

I wave airily, though my heart is thudding hard. "I always tell guys I'm waiting for marriage before having sex. That's my rule, but I think it might be time to break that rule, you know?"

He hits the gas so hard my head smacks the headrest. "Ow!"

∽

Adam

Kayla is a twenty-five-year-old virgin, and now she doesn't want to be. I do *not* need to know this. I shouldn't know this. And that rat bastard, Rob, rushed her into a wedding just so he could get sex. They were only dating two months. Kayla told me the story before. He did the full-court press—flowers, candy, cards with all that poetic love crap. And poor Kayla believed his love was true.

I glance over at her. Her head is bowed as she fiddles with the borrowed engagement ring on her finger.

I clench my jaw. And then that bastard had the balls to bring it up right in front of me just to humiliate her. "I so want to turn this car around, track that asshole down, and punch him right in his smug face."

She pulls off her sister's engagement ring and tucks it into her small beige purse. "As tempting as that sounds, I'll pass. The important thing is that he knows I've moved on."

But she hasn't. She's not seeing anyone or she would've asked someone else to step in today. She doesn't see me as a risk to her heart, which is fine because she's right. I'm never getting close enough for that to be an issue. We're both well protected in this friends thing.

She sighs. "Was it horrible for you? The party, I mean."

Actually, I felt like a rock star. She spent the whole time bragging about my skill as a craftsman. "It was fine. I didn't realize how much you absorbed about what I do."

She smiles. "I listen. While you were at the job at Wyatt's house, didn't I spend weeks asking you what you were doing and why?"

Warmth fills my chest. She always wants to know about my work and my thoughts on things. She's so smart and well read, she can talk about any topic, and the thing she seems to find most fascinating is me. "Yeah, you did."

It occurs to me I know very little about her. She's mostly asked me questions about myself. I know she studied biostatistics, that she was left at the altar, and she's a virgin wanting to change that status. Ugh, I know too much.

"I can't thank you enough for stepping up for me today," she says. "You're the best."

I glance over at her smiling face. *Beautiful.* If I had the skill, I'd paint her portrait. It's her dark glossy hair in contrast to her creamy skin, those big brown eyes, delicate cheekbones, her plump pouty lips. My gut tightens with inconvenient lust.

She crosses her legs, exposing more skin as her short skirt rides up.

Think cooling thoughts. I should try to meet someone soon. It's been a while.

We drive in silence, me trying not to notice her floral scent, the curve of her cheek. Her staring thoughtfully out the window. The only sound is the album from a band we both like, Fitz Round. It's part folk, part blues, part rock. I like the unique blend of music. Kayla likes the harmony of their voices.

She reaches forward, turning down the music. "Adam, I have a problem, and I think you might be the solution."

My mind races and then slams into the one thing I don't want her to say. *Don't go there.*

And then she says it. "My virginity has become a burden."

I keep my mouth shut.

She continues matter-of-factly, "It was a mistake to wait all these years, which is why I'd like you to help me out and take my virginity."

My heart thumps out a warning call: *danger, danger, danger.*

She sighs. "I mean, we're good friends. I trust you, so I know I have nothing to fear."·

I don't know the right thing to say here. No, obviously. But how do I explain it's not because she's not desirable—

she's too damn desirable—it's because I can't get involved with her in that way. I'm not the man she needs. She's the marrying kind. Her brother even told me that's what she's looking for in a not-so-subtle warning to keep away, which is fine because I'm never going there ever again.

"No, thank you," I say.

She stiffens. "Well, that was polite. Can I ask why?"

"No."

She slides her fingers through her hair and groans.

"Nothing personal," I say. "You should wait for the right guy, your future husband."

"That's the whole problem! I waited too long. My mom gave me this terrible advice that sex was better with love, especially married love. Now it's this giant pink V on my chest!" She thumps her chest for emphasis.

I'm about to assure her that no one would guess she's a virgin just by looking at her—I had no clue and I spend a lot of time with her—when she continues.

"My sisters told me I was missing out. They said Mom only told us to wait so we wouldn't end up pregnant and dropping out of school. It was different for my mom since she married at twenty. I'm such an idiot. Look at me, twenty-five, begging my friend to help me out. Ergh!"

I hate that she's beating herself up about it. "You're not an idiot. And it wasn't terrible advice." I know the difference when love is involved. Sometimes I wish I didn't.

"I took Mom's advice to heart and held on to it way too long. Pathetic." Her voice cracks.

I reach over and squeeze her upper arm, where she's safely covered by her shirtsleeve. "You're not pathetic."

She blinks rapidly, her lower lip quivering. *Please don't cry.* "Honestly, I didn't think waiting was a big deal before. I've never felt swept away like I had to rip my clothes off and tumble into bed like you see in the movies and TV. You know what I mean?"

I gulp. She shares way too much with me. "Yeah."

"But now it's getting in the way of my social life. It's like a conversation we need to have before things get too far. I just want it gone, and I thought…never mind." She takes in a deep, quivering breath.

"I'm sure it'll happen when the time's right." It sounds lame even to my ears. I need to stop talking about sex with her. My body's involuntary lust makes it really hard to remember why I have to keep my distance. And then she'd get hurt and it would be all my fault.

Her lips form a grim line. "I can't wait any longer. I need to take things into my own hands."

Alarm shoots through me. She sounds serious.

She starts muttering to herself about single guys she knows, and I get tenser and tenser. She pulls out her phone and starts tapping away. "Or maybe I'll try one of those hookup apps I've heard about."

I grab her phone.

"Hey!"

"No."

She gasps. "Excuse me, but you passed on my request, so it's no longer your concern."

"The hell it isn't." I shove her phone into my back pocket and focus on the road. No way she's going to have her first time with some random guy she finds online.

She purses her luscious pink lips. "I'm only doing what I feel needs to be done. I'm tired of waiting and, honestly, I'm curious what all the fuss is about."

Curious? More like reckless.

"You're fine just the way you are," I say with a note of finality. *Can we please stop talking about this?*

She's quiet, and I can almost feel the gears cranking in her brain. She's working up her next angle to fix the problem.

"Kayla, you don't have to do anything. This *thing* is not a problem." I can't bring myself to say virginity. It just feels too intimate between friends, even though she's said it plenty.

After a while, she says, "Oh-h-h, I get it now. I keep asking favors from you, and I haven't offered anything in return."

"That's not it," I mutter.

"Is there a new saw you've been eying? I imagine saws for you are like purses for me. Or I could take care of Tank, give him some cuddle time when you're away on a job. Would that help?"

"I'm not taking your damn virginity, so there's nothing you need to do!"

She huffs. "My *damn* virginity. See? I told you it was a problem. You think so too, but you're not willing to help. And I thought we were close."

I barely hold back an eye roll at her assessment. "This is why I don't have women friends. Boundaries. You're the exception because you hung out with me at your brother's place, and now we're related."

"We are *not* related!"

"Your brother married my sister."

"That's related by marriage. Eww. You think I'd want a relative to make love to me?"

Make love. My God, she's innocent. "When you're not in love, it's fucking, okay? Can you even say what it is?" I'm being snarky to make her shut up about it.

She leans close, her voice throaty and sexy as hell by my ear. "Fucking. Fuck, fuck, fuck. I want you to *fuck* me, Adam."

I go rock hard and grip the steering wheel tighter.

"We could keep it casual so no one gets hurt," she adds.

I clench my jaw against what I want to say, which is that she'll only regret sex with me. She thinks she can handle casual, but it's just not her. And there's no way in hell I'm letting her first time be with some random guy who might not treat her right. She's a good person, a *great* person, and that means she deserves someone who'll treat her like a queen. I say nothing because it's not my business.

I shouldn't even know any of this.

This is exactly why men and women can't be friends because then the woman says sex stuff and it's all the guy can think about.

I put the music back on loud, hoping she'll get the hint that I'm done talking about this topic *forever*.

Once I park in the lot of The Horseman Inn, where she lives in the apartment above, I hand over her phone. And then I can't help but say, "Don't do anything stupid."

"I know about safe sex, Adam!" She gets out of the car and stalks off, disappearing behind the restaurant, where her apartment entrance is.

I rest my forehead on the steering wheel. This is not good. I'm sorely tempted to bring Wyatt into this to shut the whole thing down. He'll lecture her and then watch her like a hawk, intervening at every opportunity. I can't. Kayla would never forgive me. But someone has to stop her.

I lift my head and put the car in gear, pulling out of the lot. I have to be the one to step in. But how can I keep her from other guys without being the prime candidate?

My lips curve up. *She chose me*. I'm not taking her up on it, but it's an honor to be chosen like that. Sweet Kayla. Of course I'll look out for her.

It hits me that all I have to do is put her off her mission for a short time. She's not going to stick around. She's looking for a job in pharmaceuticals. Then she'll move wherever her new job is, meet a fellow biostatistician or scientist type at her new company, get married, and then make nerdy love. I like thinking of her with someone nerdy. I don't know why. It's not like she's nerdy. She's a goddess.

Stall her. Now that's a plan.

3

I drive home with my next-door neighbor, Levi, around noon the next day after a relaxing Sunday morning fishing on Lake Summerdale. He's two years younger than me, longish brown hair with a beard, and our mayor. He's also a third-generation Summerdale resident (I'm fourth generation).

"Expecting company?" he asks as I pull into my driveway.

There's a red Corvette with a Florida license plate parked in front of my house. I don't know anyone from Florida. Could be a rental.

"Probably just one of our neighbors has company," I say, though an uneasy feeling rolls through me.

We get out of the car, and I open the trunk so he can grab his fishing rod and tackle box.

"Until next time," he says and heads over to his place next door.

I incline my head, shut the trunk, and make my way to the garage, tucking away my fishing gear. I had a night to sleep on it, and I feel much better about the whole *Kayla on a mission* thing. She was just upset, reacting to seeing her ex. I'm sure she'll come to her senses once she calms down, and this whole quest to get rid of her virginity won't even be an issue anymore. It hasn't been all this time, right? Things will go back to normal soon.

I unlock the door that leads to the kitchen, step inside, and freeze. There's a bouquet of flowers in a vase on the kitchen table. I didn't put that there. And Tank didn't rush to bark at me. He always barks when he hears someone come in.

"Tank?"

I hear his paws scrabbling on the hardwood floor to get to me. And then *she* steps into the room, and I go cold.

"Hello, my gorgeous fiancé!" Amelia calls, wiggling her fingers at me. Adrenaline spikes through me. My ex is back from Panama and made herself at home. Tank rushes back to her and leans his big head against her leg. That's why he didn't bark. He was probably cuddled up with Amelia. He was hers to start with as a puppy.

My voice comes out hoarse. "What are you doing here?" She's wearing a long bright orange dress with skinny straps, showing off her cleavage. There's a slit in the dress that ends by her hip, exposing her long tanned leg. All that exposed skin and I feel nothing. She destroyed everything when she cheerfully walked out the door last year.

She gestures for me to take a seat at the kitchen table, and I move in slow motion. She sits in the same spot she always did, facing the patio doors in back. Surreal. It's like she never left. Tank settles under the table, probably hoping food will appear soon.

I take a seat adjacent to her. Up close, she looks worn down. Is she sick? Is that why she came back? Her blond hair is dull and longer than it used to be, halfway down her back. She has lines around her green eyes, her entire expression fatigued. I want her out of my house, but I don't wish her harm.

"Are you okay?" I ask.

She smiles brightly. "I'm fine, thanks. Panama didn't work out."

"Okay," I say slowly.

She lifts her hands in a *ta-da* gesture. "So I'm back. And I'm very sorry I ran off like that. I truly regret my actions. I guess I got cold feet and..." She sighs, attempting to look contrite. "I've had some time to think about it and, like I said, I'm sorry."

"What happened to Gary?" That was the guy she ran off with.

"He moved on to Venezuela for his next adventure."

"And he didn't invite you?"

She frowns and quickly clears her expression. "I didn't want to go. I realized I missed you and wanted to come home."

Right. "Is that really the reason?"

"What else would it be?" She peeks under the table at Tank. "My sweet Tank. I missed you too!"

My gut clenches. "You gave him to me. He's mine now."

She looks up, smiling serenely. "He's ours. Adam, I know it will take some time, but if you can find it in your heart to forgive me, I'd really like to move back in and pick up where we left off. I kept the ring." She holds up her hand, showing me the square diamond on platinum ring that cost me three months' salary.

The shock of seeing her in my house wears off, and I'm suddenly angry. Amelia, who ripped my heart out and stomped on it on her way out the door, is acting like none of that matters. The four years we were together, our engagement, her cheating on me with some random guy from work, and taking off for Panama. And she was so damn cheerful when she left, saying she was finally with the guy who understood adventure and having a good time.

I hold out my palm. "Give me the ring."

She pulls her hand away. "It was a gift. You can't take it back."

"And I want my key."

She pouts. "Why're you being this way? Can't you even give me a chance?"

I clench my jaw, and then an idea takes hold that will both shut down any hope she has of us getting back together and give her a taste of her own callous medicine. "I'm engaged now. My new fiancée would be upset knowing you were here.

Now give me my key and the ring, and then you need to leave."

She stalks to the living room, grabs her purse, rummages through it, and produces the key. She returns to me, yanks off the ring, and drops both on the kitchen table with a clatter. "I wasn't gone that long. Who are you engaged to?"

I speak through my teeth. "You left more than a year ago." Obviously she expected me to wait for her.

"Who is it?"

"You don't know her."

She crosses her arms. "At least *I* didn't get engaged. I only had cold feet. Are you really going through with it?"

"That's the idea when you get engaged." I stand and walk to the front door, holding it open for her.

She follows me at a slower pace, stopping at the door. "I want to meet her. I need to know she's good enough for you."

"I'm no longer your concern."

"I'll find out. I'm renting a lake house with my family all summer. I'm between jobs at the moment." That's how we met. She was one of the summer people. How convenient for her to move back in with me—recently dumped, unemployed, and homeless. Not a chance in hell.

"Bye, Amelia."

I shut the door behind her and let out a breath. Talk about a blast from the past. I shove a hand through my hair. If she's here all summer, I'm going to run into her. It's not that big a town. All activity centers on the lake; all streets lead to it as well. She knows where I hang out.

An unexpectedly brilliant idea makes goose bumps break out over my skin. I was Kayla's fake fiancé in front of her ex, and she wanted to return the favor. I'll ask Kayla to be my fake fiancée this summer to keep Amelia away, which will completely eliminate any chance of Kayla hooking up with some random guy. It's the perfect solution. That is, if Kayla's still thinking along those lines.

I pull my phone from my jeans' pocket. It's like insurance or something, a safety net for my good friend Kayla. I'm a frigging genius.

I text her to see if she's up. She usually sleeps late.

Kayla: *I'm awake.*

Me: *Let's meet in front of the Horseman. I have a proposition for you.*

Kayla: *Absolutely!*

Me: *I'll drive over now.*

Kayla: *Awesome!*

I smile to myself. She's such an enthusiastic person. Sounds like she's already feeling better after her ex encounter. I'm sure she'll be a great fake fiancée for me, especially the way she always brags about me to everyone. Doesn't hurt that she looks like a goddess. Nope. Doesn't hurt at all.

Kayla

This is so exciting! Adam just needed to sleep on it, and now he's on board! I place a hand over my thundering heart. What else could a proposition mean after I asked him to take my virginity? He must want to lay out the terms so no one gets hurt. He's such a great guy.

Is it wrong I'm so excited about the prospect of sex with a guy I know doesn't want a relationship? I suppose if we both go into it knowing it's casual, it should be okay. But will it mean the end of our friendship? I hope not. Adam's a steady sort, very even-tempered, and so am I. It's a risk, but when I think about taking this step, well, only Adam will do.

What should I wear? This is big. Huge!

I rifle through my hanging rack of clothes, looking for the sexiest outfit I own. Right now I'm in a pink T-shirt and jean shorts. A dress? This pale green minidress is cute, though the top isn't too revealing with its cap sleeves and modest V-neck.

Wait, is he coming up here? I glance back at my twin-size bed with its pink and white polka-dotted comforter from home. It doesn't feel sexy enough for the big moment.

My phone chimes with a text. He's here! There's just no time!

I hurry downstairs, half afraid he'll change his mind and leave. I push through the door to the kitchen, say a quick hello to the staff, and dash out the back door.

My legs feel like quivering jelly as I round the corner of the large white clapboard house of the restaurant and bar that's both work and home for me. This old place has been The Horseman Inn since 1788. Imagine all the good times people had in the rooms upstairs when it used to be an inn. It's *finally* my turn.

I hold up a hand to wave at him and realize it's shaking. Adam cracks a rare smile that lights up his face, and I'm momentarily stunned at his masculine beauty. He's dressed casually in a gray T-shirt that stretches across his wide shoulders and faded jeans that fit him perfectly. I always knew he was handsome, sexy even, but I never let myself imagine what that could mean in a physical sense. Now it's all I can think about. I want him more than I've ever wanted anyone in my life. Somehow I just know Adam is the key to unlocking the passion within me.

I reach him, a little breathless. "Hi."

"Hey. Can we take a walk? I want some privacy."

"We could go upstairs to my place."

He looks out to the lake across the road and scans the houses for a moment. "Yeah, okay. Your place is probably best."

"Great!" I grab his hand, and he doesn't seem to mind. I guide him to the back door, and we head through the kitchen to my apartment entrance.

The cute chef, Spencer, gives me a wink and a smile as we pass like he knows what I'm up to, bringing a guy up to my room. Little does he know it's my first time ever doing this. Now that I'm taking action toward my new goal, I'm exhilarated. Getting dumped at the altar is finally behind me. I've closed that door, and I'm about to open a new one. Am I nervous? Of course. But it's Adam. My friend, my protector, my first (hopefully).

I bring Adam to my small bedroom. It's basically the only room in the apartment besides the bathroom. The living room area is used as storage for the restaurant, and I use the kitchen downstairs.

I sit on the bed and smooth out the blanket. Adam's still standing in the doorway.

"Come in," I say.

"I'm good here."

My brows scrunch together. *Is this not what I thought it was?*

His brown eyes are intent on mine. "Remember how you said you'd like to return the favor of me being your fake fiancé in front of your ex?"

"Of course." *A sex favor? Is this his subtle way of bringing up my V-card?*

He crosses his arms, his jaw clenching. "My ex showed up. I told her I was engaged, so could you be my fake fiancée?"

I smile. "I got your back." That's what he said to me when he helped me out. Adam avoids committed relationships, so this woman must be a first-class clinger.

He steps into the room, looking a lot more relaxed. "Great. I really appreciate it."

I pat the bed next to me. "Tell me your ex story so I'm prepared."

He remains standing a few feet away. "Not much to tell. She left last year, and now she's back. She wants to pick up where we left off, and I told her no."

"Where did you leave off?"

"Does it matter?"

"Of course it matters. I need to know why I should hate her."

He smiles a little before looking away. "We were engaged."

My brows shoot up in surprise. He was *engaged*? I thought he was always casual. He must avoid relationships now because of that earlier devastation. His heart is locked up tight in self-defense. I want to hug him but sense what he needs more is an ally.

"I already know she's the villain in this drama," I say. "What's her name, and what did she do to you?"

He flops down on the bed next to me and looks straight ahead. "Amelia Baxter. We were together for four years. I proposed, figuring there was no reason not to. I couldn't see us breaking up. Yeah, we fought, but we always made up."

I put an arm around his shoulders and give him a squeeze. "Four years is a long time."

He presses his lips together. "Yeah. So we were engaged, everything's rolling along with the wedding plans, oh, and she had just moved in with me too. Then, out of nowhere, she says she's leaving me. She's going on an adventure in Panama with a consultant she met at work, and would I take Tank?"

"She left her dog behind? Evil woman!"

He rests his elbows on his knees. "He couldn't have taken the tropical heat. So, yeah, that was basically it. My dad died a week later, and I went to a dark place." That was a year ago. His sister, Sydney, talks about their dad.

"Oh, Adam. I'm sorry. It sounds like you were all close to your dad."

He straightens. "Yeah, we were. After Mom died, Dad did his best to be everything we needed."

My heart aches. Adam's pain must've been horrible between losing his dad and losing his fiancée after four years together. My own *two months together and left at the altar* ordeal pales in comparison. And still it was hard for me. What a pair we are, the walking wounded, our hearts closed up tight inside. I hate to admit it, because I really am over Rob, but I still don't want to risk my heart just yet.

I lean my head against his shoulder. "You must've been devastated when all that went down." I straighten and turn to him. "You never mentioned any of this before."

He gazes into my eyes, giving me a jolt. We've never sat so close. A shimmer of awareness races over my skin.

"Adam?"

"It's hard for me to talk about."

I blink, confused for a moment. Oh, yeah, he's talking about why I'm just hearing this sad story for the first time. "I don't mind playing your fiancée. What exactly did you have in mind?" I'm good at reading him, but some things you need spelled out.

His gaze trails to my cheek, my jaw, and then my lips. Heat floods me with startling intensity. I suddenly want him to kiss me. I want him period. I've never been so certain of anything in my life.

He flops backward on the bed, staring at the ceiling. "She wants to meet you. I'm not sure she believed I'm engaged, and I really don't want to deal with her all summer. She's renting a lake house with her family. I want her to get the message and move on."

All summer? My brain starts down a very squirrely path at this revelation. I'm not sure I'll be here all summer, I could get a job soon, but if I am, then that means Adam and I will be playing an engaged couple for a decent amount of time. It's only the last week of May now. And if we're close, touching like a couple, wouldn't the next natural step be for him to be my first?

I lie down on my side next to him, propping my head on my hand. "So you want me to pretend to be your fiancée all summer?"

He turns his head to look at me. "I know it's a lot to ask. You only asked me to step in for one party. You don't have to—"

"I'll do it. Happily. On one condition."

He eyes me warily. "What?"

"That thing we talked about yesterday needs to happen."

"Kayla."

"Adam."

He opens his mouth, probably to protest, but I hold up a palm, cutting him off. "That's my only condition. It's not like I can get experience with anyone else when everyone believes we're engaged. You're basically taking me off the market for months." *And I only want you.*

"We'd tell our family the truth."

"I'm talking about single guys avoiding me because they think we're engaged. I'm not getting in bed with our family."

I shove his shoulder. "Though Drew seems nice." That's his older brother. I see him at The Horseman Inn regularly, a real badass—former Army Ranger and a blackbelt—with a heart of gold.

He jackknifes upright and narrows his eyes. "Not Drew."

I sit up too. "Calm down. I was joking."

His gaze never wavers. "How do you get that Drew's *nice*? He's grumpy with everyone."

"Because he always checks in on Sydney and asks how the restaurant business is going. That's nice. He's a good big brother."

"So am I." He sounds offended. "Just because I don't check in on her. She's a grown woman who knows her shit."

"I didn't say you weren't nice. I think you're very nice, which is why I came to you first." I smile. "This is all working out wonderfully, don't you think?" See, I can proposition too.

He faces front, looks at me and then looks again. He's definitely considering going along with my condition. I'm glad I'm fluent in Adam speak.

I feel suddenly shy. I'm not sure how to get this thing started between us, but we're already sitting on the bed. It shouldn't be too difficult. "Is now a good time for you?"

"Good time for what?"

I lean close. "We're already in bed together."

He leaps up. "I didn't agree to that."

I stand too, planting my hands on my hips. "Look, you're telling everyone we're engaged for the summer. The least you can do is actually be with me at least once to help me out." I lift my chin. "And I don't see why that can't start right now."

He looks toward the door and then back at me. "Are you saying you won't be my fake fiancée unless I hook up with you?"

"Yes."

He scrubs a hand over his face and exhales sharply.

My shoulders droop. I pushed too far. I should just tell him I'll play the part. After all, he did the same for me. The only difference is the length of time. And would it be so bad to spend the summer up close and personal with Adam?

Maybe our chemistry would land us in bed anyway. It can't all be one-sided, right?

My heart sinks as I remember the last time we played the fake-fiancé game, and I had to force him to touch me. Crap. It *is* one-sided. That's why he's hesitating.

He fixes me with a hard look, and I brace myself for the rejection, my gaze landing on his chest. "If I agree—" he starts.

My head lifts, hope bubbling up in me.

"We have to do it my way."

"Does that mean you want me too?"

"Jesus, Kayla, do you always just say stuff like that out loud?"

Is experienced Adam a bit of a prude? "Do you find me desirable?"

He steps into my personal space, his large hand cupping my cheek. That's Adam for *yes*. "My way, got it?"

I throw my arms around his neck. "Okay, we'll do it your way." It's not like I have a way. I have zero experience in this area. "What's your way?"

His thumb grazes my lower lip, his gaze heated. "It takes time for two people to get comfortable together."

My voice sounds breathy. "But I'm already comfortable with you. We talk all the time."

He pulls away. "Yes, but that's you asking about me and my work. Now it's my turn to get to know you. We need to take our time so we're both comfortable. You want me to be comfortable too, don't you?"

Now I'm getting suspicious. Is he just humoring me? I already told him I'm comfortable, and he always seems relaxed around me. "How much time?"

His gaze trails from my mouth to my breasts, to my hips, and my legs, all the way to my bare toes. I heat everywhere he looks. His head jerks up. "A lot. You need to be fully prepared. There's stages."

"Stages?" I echo breathlessly.

He steps backward toward the door. "Yeah, like stage one, perfecting the kiss. Stage two, touching, and so on. It can take a while, but it's worth it. As your friend, I owe it to you to show you the ropes. You know, the right way."

I step closer. "That sounds nice, but I'd really like to cut to the chase."

For a moment he looks panicky, and I get the distinct feeling he wants to bolt. But then he pulls himself together, saying evenly, "You can't rush it if you want it to be good."

I consider that. I do want my first time to be good, of course, but I'm also anxious to see what all the fuss is about. "How long do the stages take?"

He takes another backward step toward the door. "A month. Minimum."

"Wait! Let's start stage one now."

"My way, remember? I'll take you to dinner on Saturday for our first appearance as an engaged couple. Here at the Horseman. We need a lot of people in town to see us together. That way I know word will get back to my ex." He grins, his eyes sparkling devilishly. "Maybe she'll hate seeing me so happily engaged and move on right away."

I walk up to him. "Love the revenge angle." I give his bicep a squeeze. It's like warm marble. "And I'm looking forward to our first date."

He opens his mouth and then closes it again before turning and jogging down the stairs.

Was it the first-date part he wanted to comment on? It was his idea to spend prep time together. I'm still not convinced he needs it to feel comfortable. I mean, who's the virgin here?

He stops at the bottom of the stairs and turns to me. "Wear your sister's engagement ring."

I nod and blow him a kiss.

He shakes his head, but I catch his smile just as he turns away, pushing the door open.

This is working out better than I imagined. I just hope he doesn't make me wait too long.

~

Adam

I sit in my car for a moment, a little stunned at the turn of events. Somehow my simple fiancée plan is now complicated. And dangerous too. Sex. A date.

I let out a breath. This is my first actual date in more than a year, which somehow feels more dangerous than agreeing to show Kayla the sex ropes. Not that I plan to go through with her sex plan. I'll stall her until she leaves for her new job. As for me, I've stuck to casual hookups, though the bar scene hasn't appealed to me for months now. Ever since—

Ah, hell. What have I done?

And how am I supposed to explain all this to Wyatt?

4

Kayla

I'll admit having my first date with Adam at The Horseman Inn doesn't feel like a real date. I mean, I work here and live right upstairs. And he's been coming here his whole life. Then I remind myself this is all just part of his fake-fiancée plan, along with my plan to finally experience passion. We're helping each other out, and I did agree to do this his way.

It's Saturday night, which I usually work, but I switched shifts with another waitress and took Thursday shift instead. I missed hanging with Jenna and Audrey for Thursday Night Wine Club (ladies' night) at the bar. Sydney missed it too since she's away on her honeymoon with Wyatt in Bora Bora. Her brother Drew is managing the place in her absence since he used to run it before she took over. Super nice guy. I don't care what people say about his grumpiness.

I'm waiting in the small front foyer of the restaurant for Adam. I dressed as slutty as possible. I may be inexperienced, but I've seen how it works on TV. It was tough to find a revealing outfit in my wardrobe. What can I say? I like simple elegant clothes that never go out of style. My white with thin pink stripes dress has spaghetti straps and a V-neck emphasizing my cleavage, which I hope is tempting enough to get Adam started on the stages of seduction he promised. I added a strapless pushup bra to help in that department. There's a cinched waist, and the dress ends at the knees. Unfortunately, I'm a little chilly in the air-conditioning and sorely tempted to go back upstairs for my pink cardigan, but that would cover too much skin, so I prevail.

I've never been a seductress before. I cross my arms, attempting to warm my ice-cold hands. I'm determined to move forward despite my quivering insides. It's natural to feel nervous when trying something new, right?

Adam said we'd start on stage one tonight. That's perfecting the kiss. I still can't believe he's making me go slowly. All this anticipation is making me more nervous. I guess when you've already had sex, it doesn't seem like a big deal to wait. Now that I've decided to go for it, I want it to happen as soon as possible.

What if our first kiss is terrible?

Gosh, I hadn't considered that possibility before. It would be so awkward because then I'd have to explain we need to stop working toward my goal, no offense. That could be bad. He probably *would* take offense, and then our friendship would be ruined. He'd always be mad I thought he was a terrible kisser. Guys can really take that to heart. I may have blurted the wrong thing to a guy before just to make the sloppy kisses stop.

What if it's a great kiss? The kind with passion like you see in the movies. That kind of kiss could be wonderful. If that's the case, it's full steam ahead. I'm almost sure it will be great. There's definitely heat between us.

I brighten. If our first kiss is passionate, maybe we'll get carried away and skip ahead to the good part. I'll finally know what the fuss is about and never have to feel like a freak again. It was a real eye-opener to get a proposal just for sex. I want that off the table forever as guy incentive.

I pull my phone out of my small black Prada bag, a birthday gift from Wyatt. Five more minutes until Operation Kayla Satisfaction begins. I mean our date. *Oh, he's early!*

Didn't I say you could depend on him to honor his commitments?

Adam steps inside, his brown eyes meeting mine intently. My stomach flutters, my pulse racing. Suddenly it feels like a real first date. His eyes trail to my lips, my throat, my bare shoulders, briefly resting on my cleavage before jerking back to my eyes. Sparks fire over my skin.

"Hi." His voice sounds husky.

I smile. "Hi. You look handsome." He's wearing a navy striped button-down shirt with the sleeves rolled up, dark jeans, and dark brown leather shoes. He dressed up for our date.

His gaze roams my face from my eyes to my cheeks and finally my lips. "You too." He leans close to my ear, his voice deep and rumbling. "I like your dress."

I shiver as excitement races down my spine. Just from his deep voice so close. This is very promising.

"You cold?" he asks. "I have a fleece jacket in the car."

I shake my head. "I'm fine." I turn to the host, Sam, who just started working here on his summer break from college. "Ready for our table."

He grabs two menus and leads us toward a table for two by a window, which is great because you can see Lake Summerdale from here. Now that I live over The Horseman Inn, in the center of town, I can see how cute this planned community is. There's a lake at the center with trees surrounding it. Farther back is a ring of homes and then, like spokes on a wheel, streets leading to shops, the schools, churches, and homes. I love this town and hope I can stay. My brother's here along with his new wife, Sydney—love them both—and I have friends now. I visit Jenna's bakery, Summerdale Sweets, way too much, and I joined Audrey's book club at the library. She's a librarian and has the best taste in books. Plus I've met lots of nice people at The Horseman Inn. Everything depends on where I get a job offer though. I have applications in a bunch of places, some in New Jersey, some in New York City, one up in Boston, and one in Indiana.

Adam surprises me by pulling my chair out for me and tucking it in. Wow. Now it *really* feels like a date.

"Thank you," I murmur.

He inclines his head and takes the seat across from me.

I'm so eager I almost want to mention how much I'm looking forward to stage one. I play it cool though.

He sets his paper napkin in his lap and picks up the menu. I do the same, trying to act like a proper fiancée. If we were really engaged, we'd be totally casual on a night out.

He looks up. "New menu. Kinda fancy."

"It's the new farm-to-table concept Sydney and Wyatt put in. Quality over quantity and everything as fresh as possible." I lean forward in what I hope is an enticing display of my cleavage. "Adam?"

He glances down at my chest and gestures to it, whispering, "I can see your bra."

Good. "Have you thought about what we'll do after dinner?"

He jerks his gaze back to my eyes. "We can take a walk around the lake if you want."

"I'd love that." A romantic walk around the lake as the moon glows over the shining water. What a great date Adam has planned for us. I never considered that he might take the time to be romantic. Nice bonus!

I'm about to casually mention a kiss in the moonlight when our waitress, Ellen, a cheerful woman in her sixties, stops by to take our drink order.

She winks. "Adam, I didn't know you were taking Kayla out. Isn't she cute as a button?" She gestures toward me. "Love your dress, honey."

"Thanks," I say; then I remember our plan. I hold out my ring hand. "We're engaged."

"Oh my goodness!" she exclaims. "This is wonderful news!" She hugs Adam and then me. "Congratulations!" She looks around the restaurant; only two couples are here, seated across the room, with more people at the bar and larger groups in the back room. "Everyone, Adam and Kayla are engaged!"

The two couples in the front dining room clap politely. Ellen rushes to the bar, probably to share the news with the bartender Betsy. A few moments later, Betsy walks over to congratulate us. She's young with pink hair and multiple piercings.

Ellen joins her, and they both stand there staring at Adam with amazed smiles on their faces.

"I thought you'd never get engaged again," Betsy says.

Adam grumbles something I can't quite make out. This is the part where he's supposed to wax poetic about our love. I resist kicking him under the table.

I smile. "When it's right, it's right. Sometimes love happens when you least expect it."

Adam meets my eyes with a warm look, and it almost feels like he might have some real feeling for me. My stomach flutters, my heart picking up speed.

Ellen hitches a thumb toward him. "Guess you noticed he's the quiet type, but still waters run deep."

Betsy squeezes his shoulder. "I missed my chance with Summerdale's hottest bachelor." She winks at me.

Adam's neck pinkens.

Ellen ruffles his short brown hair, and he immediately smooths it back in place. "I've known him since he was in diapers. Sweet as they come. I'm so glad you two found each other."

She walks off, smiling.

"Congratulations again," Betsy says. "I'll send over some champagne."

"Thank you!" I say.

She walks away, wiggling her fingers in acknowledgment.

I lean forward across the table. "Smart to go somewhere they know you from diaper age. I'm sure the news will spread quickly."

He shakes his head. "Guess so. Though I think Ellen still sees me as a kid."

"She just remembers you fondly back then. I'm sure you were adorable." I lower my voice to a whisper. "By the way, I'm really looking forward to our goodnight kiss."

He does a double take, but doesn't reply. What is he thinking? It's rare I don't know. He seems almost surprised at the idea.

"Stage one, remember?" I whisper. "Perfecting the kiss. I understand it's important to warm up to the big event, so we're doing this your way. But we really shouldn't delay on getting started. Otherwise, we could waste a whole month working toward a goal that's only going to disappoint." He did say the stages would take a month minimum.

A muscle ticks in his jaw. "You won't be disappointed."

I brighten. "Have you had a lot of lovers?"

He glances around and leans across the table. "This is not appropriate conversation for a first date. I mean for an engaged couple."

I lean toward him. "Sorry. I forgot for a moment. Mmm, what's that cologne you're wearing? It smells so fresh and woodsy."

"You smell like flowers."

I grin and whisper, "So we both spritzed on enticing scents. Are you enticed, Adam?"

He leans back and returns to the menu, refusing to look at me. I glance around. We're far enough from the other couples for privacy.

I keep my voice low. "Am I coming on too strong? I'm new at seduction."

He lunges forward, his voice a fierce whisper. "Stop talking about seduction stuff. I'm the guy. That's my job."

I straighten, blinking a few times. Adam is never brusque with me like that. I must've stepped on his manly ego by accident. He wants to be the initiator. But it's been twenty-five years of waiting for me, and I'm eager to get started. Well, more like seven years, I guess, since I started seriously thinking about sex as people around me started having it. And he did lay out the stages clearly, which made me feel more confident on the path forward, like a seductress instead of an embarrassingly inexperienced woman.

I look out the window, thinking about our walk around the lake later. I swear if he doesn't make a move tonight, that is it. I'm just going to take matters into my own hands, throw my arms around his neck, and lay one on him. I need something to look forward to so I don't go crazy with all the waiting. Just a taste of passion. Is that too much to ask?

I turn back to find him looking at me expectantly. It hits me that he wants me to acknowledge his experience level in regards to being the initiator. "I'm happy to let you take the lead."

"Good."

Ellen comes back with our champagne, still exclaiming over us. I'm enjoying being his fiancée so far.

After Ellen tells us the specials, we order right away. We both know our favorites here. Adam goes with the Kobe burger, an upgrade from the old regular burger on the menu, and I go with the roast chicken and potatoes. I have breath mints in my purse for after.

I raise my glass. "To us and our everlasting happiness."

He clinks his glass against mine. "To us." We both take a drink.

His eyes meet mine for a long moment. These deep gazes are new. Is he as excited as I am about the steps of seduction? I keep quiet, allowing him to take the lead.

Finally, he says, "What do you like about biostatistics?"

Well, that's not very seductive. I really hoped he'd lead the way on this new exciting path immediately. "I'm good at it, and I like knowing my work can help people. It's very important to know what's working and not in new treatments for diseases. I analyze the data."

He keeps going, firing question after question at me in a low voice that might seem to an outsider to be romantic dinner conversation (if they couldn't hear the words clearly). Do I plan on getting a PhD? What do I do in my free time? What was it like growing up in Princeton, New Jersey? How did my older siblings treat me? Am I close with my mom? Have I ever played sports? Favorite memory? Middle name? Favorite book and movie?

It's the most he's ever asked me. And he actually seems interested that I'm not going for a PhD, enjoy reading, and binge-watching smart character-driven shows, and that I liked Princeton. I answer the rest while I eat and ask him the same, but he only wants to get to know me.

I finish dinner and give him a rueful smile, leaning close so no one can hear our private conversation. "Okay, so now you know I'm close with my family, everyone treated me well as the youngest, I was co-captain of my field hockey team, best memory was when we won the state championship, my middle name is Marie, and I love Harry Potter, the books not the movies. And I don't have a favorite movie. Can I finally get to know you now?"

A smile plays over his lips. "My middle name is Christopher."

I pretend-strangle him, and he laughs.

"You know all you need to know about me," he says. "I love my work. I love my family. You know plenty about both. Nothing else worth mentioning."

I know he lost his mom when he was a teen. I lost my dad when I was seven. We have that early parent loss in common. I don't bring it up. We both know that much about each other through our siblings.

The bill arrives, and he takes out his credit card to pay.

"Thanks for a lovely dinner, my wonderful fiancé," I say loudly.

His lips curve up. "No problem."

"I'm going to run upstairs for my cardigan before our romantic walk around the lake."

He blinks a few times, seeming surprised. Isn't that what he said we were doing?

"Just be a moment," I say and make my way through the back room, through the kitchen, and up the stairs to my place. Since I'm there, I take the time to brush my teeth before grabbing my pink cardigan.

When I get back downstairs, he stands and gestures for me to go ahead of him to the door. We step outside. It's cool now that the sun's set. I'm glad I took the time to put something warmer on.

I look out over the lake. "Oh, look, a full moon!" This is definitely a romantic sign.

"End of summer there's a moonlight regatta. Everyone rows out to the center of the lake with glow sticks, LEDs, and lanterns. It's a party."

"I want to go. That sounds amazing."

He doesn't invite me, but I'm sure if I'm still here by the end of the summer, he would.

We walk through the parking lot and cross the street to the walking path that leads around the lake. There's some sandy shoreline, but we stick further out to the tree-lined path closer to the houses.

I take his hand in mine. His hand is warm and a little rough from his work. I like it. We held hands last week too, but I was so worked up over seeing my ex I didn't really notice much about it. Now that we're working toward intimacy, I can't help but wonder what his hands would feel like on my bare skin. I'm dying to find out.

"I see you and Tank on walks out here," I say. "Always at sunset."

"He can't take the heat because of his pushed-in face. Makes it hard for him to regulate his temperature. I have to wait for it to cool off a bit."

"And then sometimes I see you carry him back to your car. He looks heavy."

"Yeah, he's a tank. Hence his name. Sometimes he'll just decide he's done walking and refuses to move."

"Are you sure he wants to go on walks?"

"It's important he gets exercise."

I shake my head. "How much does he weigh?"

"Fifty pounds." He pulls his hand from mine and flexes his bicep. "How do you think I got these?"

"The Tank workout."

"That's right."

He doesn't take my hand again, and I'm a little miffed. I step off the path to the shade of a large tree. It's time for that kiss.

He follows me. "Are you done walking? Do I need to carry you back?"

I smile. "Yes, you need to carry me back." I wait, breathless in anticipation of him sweeping me off my feet and carrying me back to the restaurant.

He goes down on one knee in front of me, giving me his back. "Climb on."

"Adam, I'm wearing a dress. I can't get a piggyback ride in a dress."

"Sure you can."

I sigh, hitch my dress up, and climb on. He stands, hooking his arms behind my bare knees. I make sure my dress is covering my ass and wrap my arms around him. Actually this is kinda nice. He's super warm and smells so good.

"Come on, little Tank," he says.

I smack his shoulder. "Never call a woman a tank."

"If she acts like a tank—"

"Don't you dare say feels like a tank."

The rumble of his laugh vibrates through his back that I'm plastered against. This is fun.

We pass a family on the way back, the parents pushing a little boy and girl in plastic toy cars. The kids honk their horns at us.

"Traffic jam," Adam says, walking around them.

"Have a good night," I call.

"You too," the parents call back to us.

"I just love this town," I tell Adam.

"Yeah, but you're leaving soon."

I sigh. "Most likely. I have to go where I can find work, but I'll definitely visit a lot. Wyatt's here. You're here."

He's quiet.

We reach the parking lot, and he sets me down next to his car. I look up at him hopefully.

He gestures toward the back of his car. "This is the part where I shove you in the back seat and put your doggie seatbelt on for you."

I laugh. "So is this the end of our date?"

"Unless you want to do something else."

"Maybe we could go back to your place, and I could say hi to Tank." *And then you could seduce me.*

"Another time."

I step closer and lift my face to his, closing my eyes. A long moment passes. He hasn't moved away. I can feel his heat, hear his breathing, smell his fresh woodsy scent. And then, finally, his big hand cups my cheek. My pulse races. He strokes my hair back, his fingers grazing the sensitive spot behind my ear.

I lean toward his hand, enjoying his touch, and then it's gone.

His lips meet my cheek in a chaste kiss. "Goodnight."

My eyes fly open. If he's going to go this slow, we need lots more dates or we'll never get there. "I'd like another date. Tomorrow. I suggest we go to your place. I'll cook."

He looks wary. "A picnic in the park would be better. I'll bring Tank. He'll be okay if we pick a shady spot."

It's not especially intimate, but he did agree to another date tomorrow. "Okay. I'll pack a picnic lunch for us from the restaurant."

He inclines his head. "You want me to walk you in?"

I gesture toward the restaurant a short walk away. "I can make it on my own."

He shoves his hands in his pockets. "Okay."

I lower my voice to a whisper. "Do you always move this slow with your dates? Just a kiss on the cheek goodnight? I kissed your cheek before this already."

"I don't have dates."

Oh no. "You're celibate?" This will not work at all. He really should've been up front with me about that. I just assumed after his fiancée devastation, he got back out there.

His eyes widen before he leans close. "Shh. Geez, Kayla, have you ever heard some things are not meant to be talked about in public?"

I let out a breath of exasperation. "It's just us."

"We're outside a restaurant where everyone in town knows me."

"So you're not celibate?" I whisper.

"Goodnight, Kayla." Translation: *no way, José*.

I hug him. "Thank you for the date. And I look forward to more." *Of the stages of seduction. Please don't make me wait a whole month!*

His arms wrap around me for a too brief moment of intoxicating warmth, his voice rumbling by my ear. "You were a great fake fiancée tonight. Thank you."

I beam. "See you tomorrow!"

I walk back to the restaurant, feeling his eyes on me. I hope that means he likes what he sees.

But when I get back to my tiny apartment and review our conversation, I start to see tonight differently. If he doesn't normally date and he's not celibate, then that means he only has hookups. So why is he insisting on a month of slow seduction with me? Am I special to him, or is he just trying to delay my goal in the hopes that I'll give up? Hmm…neither seems to fit. It must be because I'm a virgin. He's taking it slow to make sure I'm comfortable.

What a great guy!

5

Adam

I am the worst. Leading Kayla on, keeping my distance, only to turn her down in the end. I'm not going through with her sexy plan, but I don't want her with someone who won't treat her right.

I'm looking out for her as a friend. I shouldn't feel so guilty.

"Come on, Tank. Time to be a buffer." Tank is a four-year-old English bulldog with protruding lower teeth, drooly jowls, and wide haunches. He was originally Amelia's puppy when I first got together with her. She gave him to me because tropical heat and bulldogs don't get along. I love this dog. He's the only good thing from the relationship implosion. His short coat is fawn brown with white on one ear, his forehead, muzzle, and chest.

Tank doesn't move at my command. He's the laziest creature ever. Instead he looks up at me with his big brown eyes with an expression that says *again with going outside?* He's really an indoor cat. I lift him out the front door and set him down on the front lawn. He moves slowly toward my car in the driveway, where I lift him into the back seat and put his dog seatbelt on. Then I start the car and power down the windows to keep him cool.

I'm picking up Kayla and driving to the far side of the lake, where there's parkland and lots of shade for Tank. The thing is, if I don't delay Kayla's plan by at least pretending to go along with it, there are other single guys in town she could secretly approach. She seems very determined. Who knows, maybe she'd privately meet up with Spencer, the new chef Sydney hired. It would be easy to sneak him up to her room. He's not the only single guy either. The vet in town is divorced. Good guy around my age. A couple of teachers at the high school.

I turn down Lakeshore Drive. Actually, now that I think about it, Kayla often goes to Clover Park, a town over the border from us in Connecticut, when she has time off. There's a bar there with a name that makes it sound like it's crawling with single guys trolling for a pickup—Happy Endings. I always go further afield so I don't chance running into my hookups again, but Kayla—what am I doing? Making a list of potential guys to take her virginity? Hell no!

Besides, we're supposed to be engaged. The woman makes me crazy with all her sex talk. Doesn't she see she's perfect just the way she is?

I pull into The Horseman Inn parking lot, and she's already standing outside, holding a red cooler with our picnic lunch. Her hair's up in a cute ponytail, making her look even younger, sweet and innocent. *Virginal*. My heart bucks harder. She smiles and waves.

I lift a hand in greeting and park, getting out to help her with the cooler. She's in an olive green blouse that hangs loosely on her, ending at the elbows, nothing tempting there, but her black shorts are *short*. Bare silky smooth legs in flat sandals. Her toenails are painted pink.

My mouth goes dry, words failing me. All I can do is take the cooler from her and gesture toward the car.

She kisses my cheek. "Hello, stranger."

"Hi."

No danger of her falling for me with my complete lack of game. I'm usually much smoother. I can't even string together enough words for a compliment. What would I say, *great legs*? Better to keep my mouth shut.

I put the cooler in the trunk and get in the driver's side. She's already in the car, talking to Tank. "I hope you like bacon."

He leans toward her, sniffing like crazy. She holds out her palm, and he tries to lick it. She pulls her hand back, laughing, and then she meets my eyes, hers sparkling with delight.

I'm hypnotized.

"Hope it's okay to give him a little bacon," she says. "I thought he should enjoy the picnic too."

I give myself a mental shake, start the car, and pull out of the lot. "Yeah, that's fine."

"Which park are we going to? I've seen several around town, mostly on the outskirts."

"The founders made sure to preserve a lot of land when they first settled here in the sixties. I thought we'd go to the far side of the lake where there's a park."

"Oh, we could've taken a rowboat across the lake just like in a romantic movie. Do you have a life vest for Tank?"

"Yes, but it's easier to drive."

"Next time we should take a boat, get the full lake experience. If you don't have one—"

"I have one. Nearly everyone in town has a rowboat or canoe."

"I'm terrible at canoeing. I went on a field trip in high school once, and we tipped over three times. You have to balance two people just right in coordinated strokes."

My mind immediately goes to a dirty place—two people, rhythmic strokes. This is bad.

"Have you scheduled any interviews?" I ask. There. The sooner she moves to her new job, the sooner she can find a nerdy scientist type to marry and sex it up with.

"I have one in the city on Wednesday." New York City being the only city worth mentioning around here. "I'm not crazy about commuting to the city, and rent is so expensive there, so it's not my first choice. But you never know. I'm keeping an open mind. I think it's important to find a job that fits since that's where you spend most of your time, you know?"

"Yeah."

"Can I ask you a personal question?"

I tense. She's going to circle back to the sex thing. Worse than Tank with a bone. He snuffles in the back seat, probably smelling the bacon in the cooler in the trunk.

"Is it hot in here?" I ask.

"I'm comfortable. Maybe you should've worn shorts instead of jeans. Do you want to go back and change?"

"I'm fine."

She rubs the short sleeve of my black T-shirt, her soft fingers grazing my arm. "The fabric feels breathable, so I don't think the shirt's a problem."

It's definitely hot in here. I power the windows up and blast the air conditioner. I check the rearview and see Tank leaning toward the breeze from the vent.

"Tell me about all the places you applied for a job," I say.

"But I had a question for you."

"It's my turn to get to know you. Remember?"

She sighs. "Okay, but I don't see the point of telling you all the places I applied. I don't even know if they'll want me for an interview. It's a competitive process with few positions."

"Tell me anyway."

So she does, and I let out a breath of relief. Nice neutral conversation about pharmaceutical research and the kinds of treatments they're working on all over the country. One thing I learn is that she doesn't want to go too far from her family. Her mom and sister Brooke live in New Jersey, her other sister Paige lives in the city, and Wyatt is here. She wants to be within driving distance of them.

"Indiana's not driving distance," I point out.

"Eleven and a half hours," she says. "I checked. It's a short flight, though. It's not ideal, but my college roommate lives out there, so I'd have a friend at least. Anyway, that's all up in the air."

"Well, keep me posted. Every interview, every offer. I want to know."

"Really?"

"Of course."

"Okay," she says warmly. "And you keep me posted on your projects too. I just love your work."

A flush creeps up my neck. She's my biggest fan. "Thanks, I will."

She beams at me. "I'm so glad we're helping each other out like this. What are friends for, right?"

I grunt. The woman will hate me soon enough for faking her out.

∼

Kayla

Adam found a great spot under some beech and sugar maple trees for our picnic. I didn't get to ask him if he's going slow because I'm a virgin, but that's okay. I'm pretty sure that's the reason. I was hoping to talk it out, and then I could assure him I'm really fine and we don't need to go slow. In fact, going faster would probably lessen my nerves, but he seems uncomfortable talking openly about sex. Who knew the inexperienced one of us would be fine talking about it while Mr. Experience over here can't wait to change the subject?

Anyway, I do like spending time with him. Today I learned he's into fishing, and he promised to take me out for my first fishing trip. I watch as he lays out an old navy comforter for us, and Tank immediately makes himself comfortable in the center of it.

"Not so fast," Adam says, shifting him to the corner of the blanket. Tank lifts his head, makes a soft snuffling sound, and settles down again.

"Can you get lunch out?" Adam asks. "I'm going to get water for him."

"You got it." I had some help with lunch from the restaurant's new chef, Spencer. He's super flirty and cute too, but it's nothing personal. He's like that with everyone.

Soon we're settled with plates of rotisserie chicken, field

greens salad, and freshly baked baguette. Tank lifts his head, sniffing the air.

I set my plate down and get a slice of bacon from the cooler. "I didn't forget you, buddy." I crawl over to him and offer the bacon. He takes it gently from my hand and then wolfs it down. I pat his head, and he twists around to sniff my hand and tries to lick it. I pull my hand back. "Don't need a dog bath before eating, thank you very much."

I glance over my shoulder at Adam and catch him ogling my ass. I smile. Short shorts are doing the job. He whips his head away, almost like he's shy. Is he shy? He *is* quiet, but I just assumed he wasn't a big talker.

I crawl back over to him and tickle him.

He doesn't crack a smile, his eyes smoldering at me. "Not ticklish."

"I'm insanely ticklish. Don't even go there." *Touch me.*

"Noted."

I repress a sigh and settle back with my lunch, turning to the view of the gently lapping lake. There's a few Sunfish boats out there in the distance with bright white sails, along with a pair of kayaks. Probably more people are on the opposite shore around the bend.

Adam's quiet, so I have plenty of time to think about next steps. If he's shy, he won't be quick to seduce..On the other hand, if all he has are hookups, then he must know how to close the deal, so to speak. It's a paradox. I really wish I knew what was going on in his head. I thought I knew him so well before we entered sexy territory.

"What are you thinking about?" I ask.

"Nothing at all."

"I'm thinking about you. You're a paradox. You implied you only have hookups since your broken engagement, yet—"

"Tell me what it was like growing up the youngest of the family."

He always asks me about myself when he doesn't want to talk about himself. Welp, if it makes him feel more comfortable seducing me, I guess I can share. So I tell him about

Wyatt and how he was kinda like a dad to me after our dad died. He taught me to ride a bike and gave me loads of advice about school and also taught me self-defense. Then there's my oldest sister, Paige, who used to boss me endlessly, but still lent me her favorite dress for my eighth-grade dance. Brooke and Paige used to fight like cats and dogs and then confided in little me how horrible the other girl was. I was just happy to be included.

"Cool," he says.

That's all he says after I shared all the way through lunch. I put our dishes back in the cooler and throw out the leftover bits of food in a garbage can across the way by the bike path.

When I get back, Adam's lying on his back, his hands behind his head, looking up at the sky through the tree branches. His dark green T-shirt stretches enticingly across his chest. I'm tempted to lie next to him, but I have a feeling he'd sit up immediately. Instead I pluck a buttercup and take a seat next to him, sitting with my legs crisscrossed.

"For you, shy guy." I slide the flower into his hair right above his ear.

He grabs it and sits up, staring at it. "You put a flower in my hair?"

I nod.

He slides it into my hair above my ear. "Guys don't wear flowers. And I'm not shy."

I shift to look at him, our eyes meeting up close. My breath hitches. There's golden specks in the brown irises of his eyes. "Good."

His gaze drops to my mouth. "What's good?"

I slide my fingers into the soft hair at the nape of his neck. "That you're not shy."

His head lowers, and I close my eyes, nearly vibrating in anticipation. He places a soft kiss on the corner of my mouth. A jolt goes through me at the touch.

"Adam?" a feminine voice says.

He stiffens and slowly turns toward a pretty woman with long blond hair, wearing a red tank top, denim shorts, and flip-flops. She's standing at the edge of our blanket. "Hey, Amelia."

It's the villainous ex who broke off their engagement to run away with another guy to Panama! I immediately move into adoring-fiancée mode, leaning against Adam's side.

She pushes her white-framed sunglasses up and stares at me while talking to Adam. "I was driving by and thought I recognized your car." She flashes a smile that doesn't reach her eyes. "You must be the new fiancée."

I smile and hold up my hand to show off my sister's sparkly diamond engagement ring. "That's me. I'm Kayla. Nice to meet you, Amelia."

Her lips purse. "How long were you dating before he proposed?"

I turn to Adam, smiling. His turn to answer.

Adam takes my hand, entwining our fingers together. "Why does it matter? We're engaged. End of story."

She crouches down to rub Tank's big side, where he's sleeping. "Guess a quick proposal points to a rush. You were never one to rush, Adam. It's one of the things I liked best about you. The way you take your time guarantees *satisfaction*." Her voice sounds husky on that last part.

I narrow my eyes. She's playing the sex card, reminding us both what they had. "I certainly have no complaints in the bedroom." *Because we haven't made it there yet. Ha-ha.*

She huffs and rises to her feet. "So crass."

Adam grins. "Kayla's very open and honest. It's one of the things I like best about her."

Unlike you, cheater Amelia!

"Aww, thank you." I give him a soft kiss on the lips and instantly want more. Our gazes collide in a moment of electric attraction. This is *so* happening.

Tank whimpers. I look over, and Amelia is striding back to a red Corvette.

"I think your plan worked," I say.

He watches her leave. "You don't know Amelia. She's in sales and knows how to be aggressive to close the deal."

"Is that how she closed the deal with you?"

We both watch as her car roars off down the road.

"Not at all. It was casual between us for the summer, and then I followed up. She played hard to get, and it only made me pursue her more. I never saw her for what she really was. Manipulative, careless about people—"

"And her dog."

He looks over at Tank. "He was collateral damage in her quest for adventure. She wouldn't have been happy with me long term, so I guess, in hindsight, it was for the best."

I wrap my arms around his middle and hug him. He drapes an arm around my shoulders and kisses the top of my head. It's so unfair to him to be blindsided like that after four years as a couple.

I lean back to look at him. "I hate that she hurt you."

He tucks a lock of hair behind my ear. "I survived."

"Do you think she moved on, or should we keep doing the engaged-couple thing?"

The backs of his fingertips graze my cheek. "We have to do it all summer because that's how long she's here. If she thought we broke up, she'd probably show up at my place again."

My eyes widen. "Again?"

He traces a line down the side of my neck, leaving a tingly trail that makes it hard to focus. "Yeah, she still had my key and let herself in last Sunday."

I blink a few times. "Wait. She broke into your house? She sounds off. Why wouldn't she just call or knock on the door to be invited in?"

His words run hot over my lips. "I don't want to talk about her."

My breath hitches a second before his mouth covers mine in a whisper of a kiss. His hand cups the back of my neck as he deepens the kiss, fitting his lips to mine more firmly, and then another kiss and another. Each kiss finding the perfect angle to how we fit together. Electric heat floods me.

And then he's lowering me to the blanket, his fingers spearing through my hair as his lips press harder, opening me to his exploration, his tongue thrusting inside. I wrap my arms around him, stroking his broad back and shoulders, aching to feel his weight on me. He holds himself over me, his kisses becoming more demanding. Raw lust races through me in a dizzying rush. This is the passion I've craved. Desire pools low in my belly; an instinctive need to get closer has me pulling at his shoulders, craving full-body contact.

He breaks the kiss, both of us breathing hard. His forehead drops to mine, his eyes closing. "Kayla."

"Stage one unlocked," I whisper. "We perfected the kiss. Now it's time for touching."

He groans and sits up. "I should take Tank for a walk."

"Not yet."

He glances down at himself, muttering, "Yeah, I'll wait." He's got a sizable bulge in his jeans.

I make my way over to straddle his lap and grin. "Now no one can see."

He groans, his hands going to my waist. "You're not helping."

I kiss him. He grips my hair, sucking on my lower lip before claiming my mouth. *Yes!* I so wanted this. Him. My hips instinctively shift against him, seeking friction. A rush of pleasure goes through me on contact.

Suddenly I'm airborne as he lifts me off him and sets me on the blanket.

Never piss off a frustrated virgin.

I narrow my eyes. "Do not even tell me this is how you seduce your hookups. You're holding out on me, and I want to know why."

He puts his hands on my shoulders in a bracing grip, his voice low. "We agreed to take it slow, a month minimum. Two months is even better."

"No, it is *not* better. I want you. And I know you want me."

He closes his eyes. "This is only day two. There's no rush."

I'm not remotely satisfied with that answer. Also, his hands on my shoulders are kinda holding me now, and I like it. "I think it's important we keep going for intimacy compatibility. Otherwise, it could be awkward and not so good by the time we make it to bed."

I'm flying by the seat of my pants here, throwing out what I hope sounds like a reasonable suggestion to keep this thing going. *Yes, that's me. Clueless but optimistic.*

His fingers grip my shoulders tighter. "*Intimacy* compatibility? You can't even say the word. This is why slow makes sense."

Of course I can say it. It's just new to me, but I'm open to it now. "Sexual compatibility. We need to know if we're compatible *sexually*."

His fingers slide over my shoulders in a caress, his gaze caught on my mouth. "I'm not worried about that."

"Kiss me, touch me, do everything the way you do for your hookups. Like all you care about is tumbling into bed." I *so* want to be that for him. The kind of woman you lust for so powerfully you just can't wait for more.

He pulls me into a hug, his arms wrapping around me. "I'm treating you better than that."

I want to smack him in pure frustration, but it feels wonderful to be held so close in his strong arms. Heat builds between our bodies. I know we're compatible. I just want more. I lift my head, and the moment I do, he releases me, heading over to Tank.

He clips the leash to Tank's harness. "Time for a walk." Tank takes his time getting up and stretching.

I take the flower from behind my ear and roll it between my fingers. On Adam's watch I'm going to die a virgin.

I'm beginning to suspect that's his plan.

The next day is Monday, which is always my day off since The Horseman Inn is closed. I stop by Summerdale Sweets, Jenna's shop, for a late breakfast. It's around eleven, usually a quiet time of morning, which is good because I really need to talk to her.

I open the door, and the bell jingles above it. "Morning," I call.

"Practically noon," she says, handing over a box tied with string to a brunette woman in her thirties. "Thanks. Have a good day."

I approach the counter, and my mouth waters as I look over the glass case of cupcakes, cookies, brownies, and various sweet layered bars. "I'll take a carrot cupcake and a bottled water. That sounds like a healthy breakfast."

Jenna smiles. "Absolutely." She's physically the opposite of me, tall and lean with blond hair that just brushes her shoulders. Her eyes are a pretty green. I'm dark-haired, short and curvy. Audrey's like me, actually. We could pass as sisters.

I watch her get my breakfast in her cute white scoop-neck blouse and skinny jeans. "I still don't know how you can bake all this delicious stuff and never gain weight."

"Don't hate me," she says, putting the carrot cupcake on a

small plate. "It's my high metabolism. I can eat whatever I want."

"Braggart."

She hands over the cupcake and water, and I pay her.

A chime goes off, and she turns to answer the back door. A handsome delivery guy steps inside holding a large box. His teeth flash white against his dark skin, and you'd have to be dead to miss his spectacular body encased in a snug uniform of short-sleeved shirt and shorts.

"I got what you ordered, Jenna," he says in a deep baritone voice full of innuendo.

Jenna puts a hand on her hip and responds, "You know where to put it."

He chuckles low and turns to put the box in a back storeroom. The sparks flying between them are obvious from here. She follows him, standing in the doorway, chatting.

I can't hear what she's saying, but I bet it's more flirty seduction. I so need to know her secrets.

She backs out of the doorway as he moves forward, a dance of sorts, where they're close but not touching.

He gives her a sexy smile. "Until next time."

She wiggles her fingers at him. The moment the door closes behind him, she turns and fans herself.

"What was that?" I ask. "Who was that?"

She grabs a bottled water, walks around the counter, and gestures for me to take a seat. There's three small round tables at the front of the shop. Large windows with cute awnings offer a view of the downtown—the post office, a small grocery store, The Horseman Inn, and two churches at either end.

I take the table farthest from the door and peel the wrapper off my cupcake.

"That was Trey," she says, unscrewing the cap of her water and taking a drink.

I take a bite of cupcake, the cream-cheese frosting melting in my mouth. I wait eagerly for the whole story, gesturing her on.

She sets her water down, a small smile on her lips. "We had a thing once. It's over."

"Just once? Why is it over? There's so many sparks between you two."

She shakes her head. "Any guy you sleep with will have sparks with you. Of course, I only sleep with guys I have sparks with, so maybe it's a chicken and an egg thing."

Huh?

She sighs. "He's a great guy, but I told him up front it was a onetime thing, and he respects that. Now we just have this little flirty reminder. It's fun."

I take another bite of cupcake and chew. "Wouldn't it be more fun to keep hooking up?"

She shudders. "That's a slippery slope to a relationship. I only want casual. It's better to meet different people, have lots of different experiences."

"So you never want to settle down and get married?"

She grimaces. "Nope. It's not for everyone."

I know I want that one day, but first I need to get some experience like she said. I finish my cupcake off just as she says, "What's new with you?"

I take a deep breath. I've been hanging with Jenna, Audrey, and Sydney for more than two months now. I think I can trust her with this. "I need some advice about a guy."

She leans in. "Ooh, who is it? That hot chef?"

I shake my head. "The thing is, I need to know how to let a guy know it's time to have sex."

"Which guy?"

"I don't want to say just yet, okay?" I sense Adam wouldn't want people knowing he said he'd take my virginity. He's a very private, reserved guy, and he's already told me not to talk about sex stuff publicly. This doesn't count though; we have the sisterhood code in play.

She sighs. "Fine, but I'm keeping an eye on you. I'll figure it out."

"If you do, keep it quiet, okay?"

She chews her lower lip thoughtfully. "I'm so intrigued.

It's not Drew, is it? I've seen you talk to him at the restaurant. Audrey has a thing for him, so it might be awkward."

My eyes widen. *How did I miss this?* "She does? But I keep seeing her on dates from eLoveMatch at the restaurant."

"First dates only. No one can live up to Drew."

"Does he know?"

"If he doesn't, he's an idiot." She nudges my arm. "Now what's the situation with your guy? How long have you been seeing him?"

I neatly fold my cupcake wrapper, a little embarrassed at how little progress we've made together. "We've been on a couple of dates, and we only kissed once." I risk a glance at her. She's not laughing; instead she looks thoughtful.

"Did you like it?"

"Yes, but I need more. And it seems like the more I talk about moving to the bedroom, the less he wants to do anything."

She squeezes my arm. "Oh, sweetie, you don't need to talk a guy into sex. It's so easy. You just stand close, touch him, and smile. He'll get the message."

"Is that what you did with Trey?"

"That's what I do with all guys."

"How do you touch him?"

Her brows shoot up. "How?"

"Yes. Is it a squeeze or a stroke? On his arm, hand, what?"

"Anywhere. Stroke his shoulder, bicep, hand, or you could just place your palm flat on his chest. That's a good spot that always gets their attention."

"Wow. Good to know. The sexy chest move."

She leans in, her voice dropping to a whisper. "Haven't you ever been with a guy? I thought you were engaged before."

"Promise you won't share this with anyone—"

"Oh my God, you're a virgin!"

I close my eyes, my cheeks burning. Thank goodness we're alone in the shop. "Yes. And I no longer want to be. I found a guy who says he's willing to help me out—he knows the deal—but he's being so slow about it."

"You found a guy," she echoes. "Is it Adam? I know you two hang out."

I fight back a blush. "I really can't say."

She smiles knowingly. "Total sweetheart. He's being kind, knowing you're a virgin. You poor thing. You must have so much built-up tension."

"Not exactly. I just want to see what all the fuss is about."

She taps her finger against her lips. "My advice is to stop talking about it and just use your body to let him know you're ready. Most importantly, touch him while holding eye contact. It's pretty universal. All guys will respond to that."

"Thanks, Jenna. I'm going to try that."

She gives me a fist bump. "I can't wait to hear how it turns out."

The bell jingles as a young mom comes in with a baby on her hip.

"Back to work," Jenna whispers. "Good luck!"

"Thanks."

"Worst case, I've got a great app you can try for just this kind of situation," she says over her shoulder. "I'll text you the link."

"Okay, thanks." She means a hookup app, which I'm not keen on anymore. Not that I was ever seriously into it. I was just throwing out options when I first came up with the idea to lose my V-card. It has to be Adam. I just need to give him the message that I'm ready.

I leave with a bounce in my step. Jenna was the perfect person to talk to from my local friends. I'm close with my new sister-in-law, Sydney, too, and now that she's back from her honeymoon, I could've talked to her about my problem, but I worry she'll slip and say something to Wyatt. He'll intervene, doing his overprotective big-brother thing. I don't think Audrey would be all that helpful. How much seducing could she be doing when she tells every guy goodbye after the first date?

≈

I decide to set my new seduction plan into motion when Adam's done work tonight. I need to try out some of those subtler techniques Jenna told me about. Now that I think about it, of course words didn't work on Adam. He's a man of action, not words. This will be the third day in a row we see each other, but I'm not worried it's too much because he's the one who wanted to see me for a month first. Maybe I'll wear him down in a week or so, and then we can get to the good part.

In the meantime, I'm going to window-shop over in Clover Park, about a half hour away. They have this fantastic Main Street I like to cruise.

I park my red Jeep in a small lot tucked on a side street and head to my favorite destination, Book It. The first time I visited Clover Park with Sydney, we went to Shane's Scoops for hand-made ice cream. We met the owner, Shane, himself, a cheerful red-haired guy who gave us coupons to shop at Book It for ten percent off. His wife, Rachel, runs the bookshop. Now I'm a member of Book It's frequent buyer club and get even more discounts.

Rachel's behind the counter. She's probably in her forties with glasses and dark brown hair that just brushes her shoulders. Her black T-shirt says *Readers Rock*. My kind of woman. She looks up, meeting my eyes with a smile. "Hi, Kayla, let me know if I can help you find anything."

"Okay, thanks! Doing my usual browse."

Just then two red-haired girls barrel through the door. They're close in age, maybe thirteen or fourteen, and I wonder for a moment if they're twins. But one girl has hazel eyes and the other blue, and they're not quite the same height. They're dressed casually in T-shirts and shorts.

"Mom, can we get money for pizza?" one asks.

"We're starving!" the other says, nodding vigorously.

Rachel gestures them closer and kisses each of them on the forehead. "Hello, Abby, hello, Hannah, how was school today?"

"Hi, Mom," they say in contrite unison. A subtle reminder of manners from Mom over here.

"School was fine. We're hungry," one says.

"I did my homework already," the other says.

Rachel reaches for her purse and pulls out a twenty. "I want change, girls."

"Thanks, Mom!" they chorus in unison and bolt out the door.

They remind me of me and my sisters. I should call them. I browse the front displays and make my way to the back to personal growth. Maybe a sex book would help. Then my eye catches on a very sexy display off to my left. A romance section with a large selection of Fierce trilogy books by Catherine Cliff—*Fierce Longing, Fierce Craving, Fierce Loving.* Well, I'm definitely experiencing fierce longing. They made movies out of the books too, starring Claire Jordan. Supposed to be pretty racy. Couldn't hurt, right? And some of them have stickers that say autographed copy. Cool. I get the whole trilogy.

I go to the front counter, slightly embarrassed to be buying a pile of sexy books. I've never done this before. I usually read literary books, something Audrey and I have in common.

"Good choice," Rachel says brightly. "The author is local, so we often get her books signed. You'll love them."

"It's my first time reading a romance."

"Oh, we have a great selection. If you like these, I can recommend more by her and other authors the next time you come in."

And just like that, I'm not embarrassed in the least. This is great. I'm an openly sexual woman exploring my sexuality. Soon to actually have sex.

I smile and hand her my credit card. "Thanks so much."

I pay and say goodbye, my eye catching on a toy store down the street. They have a large red wagon in the window with a plush teddy bear sitting in it. I know who would like that.

I drop my books off at my car and go down the block to the toy store. Even better, when I get to the wagon section, I find a wagon with an awning shade and a clip-on fan. Perfect.

I buy it on the spot and pull my car around behind the shop for one of the employees to help load it into my car.

Adam

Kayla texted earlier, telling me to let her know when I take Tank on his walk tonight. She's really taking this dating for a month seriously, wanting to meet up with me every day. I hope she's not going to bring up more sex talk. I'm happy to see her in public as much as she wants. That way there's no risk. I like spending time with her, and the more I get to know her, the more time I want to spend with her. I'm being careful not to get too attached though. I'm just enjoying her company like friends who see each other every day.

Here I am in my usual spot at The Horseman Inn, ready to take Tank on his sunset walk. I take him out of the car and snap his leash on. Then I text her.

A few minutes later, she appears, popping out the front door, and holding up a finger for me to wait. I watch as she goes behind the restaurant. What's she up to? She reappears pulling a red plastic wagon with a white shade on top.

She smiles. "It's for Tank. That way you don't have to lug him back on his walks." Tank goes right up to her, sniffing the pockets of her beige shorts. They're not super short this time. His nose goes into her crotch, and she pushes him away with a laugh. "Yes, I'm still a girl."

I tug Tank away and stare at the wagon. There's a little fan attached to the awning support. She bought my dog a present with her measly waitress salary. She never takes money from her wealthy brother. She wants to earn it.

I clear my throat over an unexpected lump of emotion. "Thanks. You didn't have to do that."

"I know. I wanted to. I'll go on the walk with you, and when he gets to the point where he decides he's done walking, I'll lure him in."

She smiles, and a surge of affection goes through me. I fight the urge to hug her. It's just such a sweet gesture to get

Tank a present. I restrain myself. The less I touch her, the easier it is to keep my distance. I can't let myself get too close. She's my friend, who's leaving soon. A really awesome, sweet, beautiful woman friend.

She pats her pocket. "I have bacon in a sandwich bag in my pocket for him."

I realize with a start that I'm just standing here smiling like an idiot. I gesture for us to go on our walk. She fills me in on her day and how much she likes the shops over at Clover Park. She even shares that she's started reading the Fierce trilogy.

I don't comment on that, even though I know it's a racy movie. I prefer not to talk about sex with Kayla. My main goal is to give her friendly dates and chaste kisses until she moves to wherever her new job takes her. I'm sure she'll get a job offer soon. She's brilliant. If I fail, cross a line that can't be uncrossed, it's not just Kayla who will end up hurt. She already means too much to me. It'll be tough to say goodbye. Not to mention Wyatt will raise hell after he warned me away.

Tank does his usual flop down on the ground halfway back, refusing to walk any farther. Kayla leaps into action, holding a bit of bacon by his nose and leading him forward, dropping more bacon in the wagon. He falls for it. He'll do anything for food. Kayla opens the hinged door on the wagon's side, but Tank can't fit. I lift him and set him down inside. He immediately wolfs down the bacon waiting there for him.

Kayla turns the fan on, and Tank lifts his head, licking his chops and looking happy. His jowls blow back a bit in the breeze. So damn cute this dog.

"Now we move nice and slow," she says, starting to pull the wagon. Tank looks alarmed for a moment, but Kayla praises him and gives him more bacon.

Within minutes, Tank's having a great ride back in his covered wagon with a motorized breeze. He even lies down, resting his head on the bench seat in front of him.

"It worked!" she exclaims.

"You know he's always going to want a ride now."

"You might need a little treat in your hand to encourage the walk before you give in and let him ride. That way he still gets his exercise. Ooh, I know. Put a big teddy bear in the wagon like it's his turn first."

"Yeah, I'm not carting a stuffed teddy bear around. I'll figure something out."

She giggles. "But it would be so cute!"

When we get back to The Horseman Inn, I lift Tank out of the wagon and set him on the ground. He immediately goes to Kayla and leans against her leg.

Kayla rubs his head. "You liked that, didn't you, Tank?" She shifts uncomfortably. "Ooh, you're heavy."

He looks up at her like he wants to keep her.

I'm starting to feel the same way.

"Okay if we hang out tonight?" she asks. "I don't have a TV at my place, but maybe we could go to your place and—"

"Sure." I don't even have to think about it. I want to spend more time with her.

Friends hang out. It's fine.

7

Kayla

Now this is progress. Already on date three, and I've moved it to private quarters. Adam's house is at the opposite end of town as The Horseman Inn, so it's the first time I've seen his place. It's a two-story beige colonial with black trim on a leafy suburban street, one of the spokes of the town wheel. He says he got it for a steal because it needed renovations, which he was happy to do. He's very handy, apparently, and could be a general contractor but prefers carpentry work. He says most of the homes away from the lake were built in the nineteen seventies. The lakeside homes are circa nineteen sixties.

He lets me in to a small foyer. On the left is a dining room with a fireplace and a gorgeous warm brown wood dining table with tapered splayed legs and upholstered black chairs. On my right is a large living room that looks comfortable with a cushy gray sectional sofa and more warm brown wood furniture—a coffee table with two drawers and splayed legs like the dining room table and two end tables with a shelf underneath.

Tank ambles over to a dark green plaid dog bed next to the sofa in the living room.

"Did you make this gorgeous wood furniture?" I ask.

A smile plays over his lips. "Yeah. It's walnut."

I wander over to the dining room and run my hand over the smooth finish. "Spectacular."

"Thanks. You want a drink?"

"Sure." I follow him to the kitchen, where it's clear he's made updates with modern-looking cabinets, this time in a light wood, with black appliances. The counters are white. "You have great taste. I'd have you do my home if I had one."

He mutters a thanks and opens the refrigerator. "Beer?"

"I'll just have water."

"Thought so," he says, getting two glasses of water for us.

I follow him back to the living room. He hands me the glass and sets out two wood coasters with metal trim. "Did you make the coasters too?"

"Nope. Bought those."

We both take sips of water and set them on the coasters. I'm about to make my hand-on-chest sexy move when he leans away and grabs the remote off the end table.

"What do you want to watch?" he asks, turning on the flat-screen TV mounted on the wall across from us. It's right above the fireplace.

I'd like to watch you. Naked.

"What do you usually watch?" I ask.

"Yankees if they're on. Sometimes a car show."

I gesture toward the TV. "Go ahead and put on what you like."

He puts on the Yankees. That's fine. It will give me better focus. I debate holding his hand, but we've done that before, and we never progressed far from that.

I wait until he leans back into the sofa. Then I lean sideways into the cushion next to him and gently place my hand on his chest right over his heart. Wow. I can feel it thumping hard. His heart must be powerful.

A long moment passes, where I'm overly conscious of my own breathing. He's not pushing my hand away, but he's not getting my sexy message either. Then he does something strange. He taps his toe sharply on the hardwood floor.

Tank hurries over, sniffing the ground like crazy. After a

few moments, Tank looks up at us expectantly. Adam pets him and then hauls him up on the sofa next to him.

I reach across Adam to pet Tank, brushing against Adam, and he shifts back so we don't touch at all. So he's using his dog as a buffer, huh? Clearly, Adam has *no* intention of helping me out. I don't know what his game is, but it's time for me to take charge. I cannot believe the virgin is the one who has to take charge here. Seriously.

"Adam, what would you consider the best way to seduce someone?"

He pulls at the collar of his blue T-shirt, looking uncomfortable.

"I'm asking you as a knowledgeable guy friend." I say this as if he might be helping me out for future guys, which always gets a quick reaction from him. I sense he doesn't want me with any guy ever—not him, not someone else. He wants me to stay a virgin, out of misguided kindness. Of course I appreciate him looking out for me, but I know what I want. Him.

He swallows audibly. That's Adam for *oh, shit. She's pushing the sex thing*. And I know Jenna told me to use action, not words, but it didn't work! I have to get the answers from the man holding out on me.

I continue. "How do you signal subtly to your partner? I mean, I don't always want to announce I want to have sex. What do you think works best for guys? Not you, just in general."

That gets him talking, as I knew it would. I keep a straight face.

He shakes his head. "Guys don't need to be seduced at all."

"Surely they need some kind of signal?"

"Nope."

I shift toward him. "Okay, then, how about the opposite? What do women need to be seduced? I've never experienced it either way since I'm always up front about waiting for marriage. Now I want to know."

He coughs. "Uh…"

I press on. "I could ask my sisters, but they'd tease me mercilessly, and Sydney is with my brother, and I don't like to imagine it, frankly."

He makes a weird gurgling sound. "I don't like to imagine it either."

"But surely you have experience seducing women."

Another cough.

He's not very forthcoming.

I imagine it for him. "If I were being seduced, I'd like flowers followed by champagne, no, wine, for the perfect seduction scene. Maybe some nice music that we both like, sung by a guy with a deep voice. Some kind of thumping bass beat could be sexy." I check in with him to see if I'm on the right track.

"Huh."

Good enough. "So then it's kiss, feel the body, and maybe unbutton your shirt, just a small reveal. But how do you know it's the right time for a reveal? I don't want to embarrass myself doing that prematurely. What if I start to strip, and he was thinking it was time to end the date and say goodnight?"

His jaw works for a moment before he finally says, "If you strip, he's on board. If he strips first, run."

I smile, pleased he's finally joining me in this illuminating conversation, but then I frown. "That doesn't make sense. Why do I run if he strips, but he stays if I strip?"

His brown eyes are intent on mine. "Look, it's a mutual thing, and you'll just know when the time is right. Okay?"

I lick my lips, and he watches the movement. "Okay."

Tank lays his head on Adam's lap, and Adam shifts before picking him up and putting him back in his dog bed. My pulse races. Does that mean the Tank buffer is gone?

I realize Adam hasn't watched the baseball game on TV very much. I must be more interesting than baseball. Jenna's advice replays in my mind: *just stand close, touch him, and smile. He'll get the message.* Never mind that her chest move didn't work. I have to keep trying her stuff. I don't have any moves of my own.

I stand, crossing to him on his way back to his spot on the sofa, and step close. Then I touch his arm, look up, and smile. *I'd still like you to be my first,* I say telepathically.

His voice is hoarse. "This is a bad idea."

"Which part?"

He hauls me against him and kisses me. A dizzying rush of lust makes my knees weak. His hand cups the back of my head, his mouth moving over mine expertly, his tongue spearing inside to taste. My fingers clutch his shirt, heat roaring through me, an insistent throbbing between my legs making me instinctively press closer, my hips lifting to meet an impressive erection.

He pulls away abruptly, breathing hard. "You should go."

I reach for him, but he steps back. This pisses me off to no end. He gave me a taste of passion, and now he's taking it away. "I wasn't done."

"Goodnight, Kayla."

I huff and stalk over to the end of the sofa to grab my purse. "I know you think you're protecting me by keeping me at a distance, but there's nothing to protect me from here." I face him. "I trust you. And I know you'd never intentionally hurt me, but this pushing me away is starting to hurt."

He shoves a hand through his hair. "Kayla, I feel *really* strongly that marriage is the commitment needed for this next step you're so eager for. You were right all along."

My jaw drops, and I shut it with a snap. This is exactly the problem. Guys see me as the wholesome girl you marry, not the kind you have fun with. Not that Adam's proposing. I know he's not ready for that kind of commitment. He just believes that's what I need.

I'm going to let him know exactly where I stand in my subtle way, as though he's just proposed.

I give his arm a gentle squeeze. "I'm very sorry, but I can't marry you just for sex. I'm not right for you anyway. I'm very talkative, and you prefer quiet. I like character-driven dramas; you like boring baseball. I love to dance and have fun at parties; you like to work your wood." He makes an odd gurgling sound, but I press on. "We have nothing in common besides our siblings. Though I'll be honest and say I do think your butt is perfection in jeans. But that's not enough to base a marriage on."

I wait, searching his expression, which is hard to read. Does he understand we don't have to get to marriage level of commitment to move forward with my goal?

"Okay," he murmurs.

I smile weakly. I don't think he got the message. I played up our differences, but we do have stuff in common. Our temperaments are well matched; we have chemistry and, importantly, respect for each other.

We actually might fit perfectly together. Me and Adam, a real couple. Mind blown.

Tank starts barking, rushing through the kitchen. A moment later, Amelia appears, a wild look in her eyes. She pulls Tank close against her side and faces us. Her long blond hair is tied back, and she's wearing a cropped white top with frayed jean shorts and hiking boots.

I go cold. This woman is a stalker and an intruder as well. I pull my phone from my purse. "I'm calling the police. Breaking and entering."

Adam holds a palm up to me. "Hold on that. Amelia, how did you get in here? Did you make copies of my house key?"

She scoffs. "I know the code for the garage door opener. It's not hard. Your mother's birthday."

Adam mutters a curse. "I'll be changing that. What do you want?"

She glares at me. "You don't belong here. This is my and Adam's house."

"He's engaged to me," I say evenly.

She lifts her chin and turns to Adam. "So you get everything and I get nothing? Just because of one mistake? Now you get the wedding, the house—"

"This was always my house," Adam says. "I paid for it. You were invited to move in with me, and then you left."

Her eyes dart around the room, and then she looks to Tank leaning against her side. "Then I get him. I have his papers from the breeder. I bought him as a puppy. He's mine."

Adam steps closer and pats his leg. Tank wanders over to him. He grabs his harness. "You gave him to me when you left."

"You can't prove that."

"Where would you even take him?" Adam asks. "As far as I know, you don't have a job, and you're staying with your parents."

"I'll keep him at my parents' place."

"I'll pay for him. Is that what you need, money?"

Amelia glances at me and then turns to him. "Four thousand dollars. That's what I paid for him. No, make it five. Inflation."

I gasp. "You can't seriously be extorting five thousand dollars out of him."

Adam holds his palm up. "I don't have it. I can give you one thousand, but you need to sign something saying you give up all rights to him. And you can never see me again. Deal?"

"No deal," she snaps, turns on her heel, and marches back out the way she came in, taking the interior door through the garage.

I stare at Adam in astonishment. "That's the woman you fell in love with?"

He scrubs a hand over his face. "She's desperate. I don't know what's going on with her, but it's not my problem."

"I don't think she's going to just go away."

"I wish she would."

"You should call Eli and get a restraining order against her. She's let herself into your house twice now uninvited." Eli is a cop in town and his brother.

He shakes his head. "I'll just change the garage code. It's fine. She's not dangerous."

It strikes me that Adam is entirely too forgiving.

"She doesn't deserve you," I say.

He stares at me for a long moment before shaking his head. "I'm going to change the code. Don't worry about her."

"What if she gets jealous and comes after me?"

"I told you she's not dangerous. You're fine. She's just upset because things didn't work out with the guy in Panama, and now she's come home to nothing. She'll land on her feet somewhere."

"File a restraining order."

He walks over to me, cups the back of my head, and kisses my forehead. Then he walks through the kitchen, presumably toward the door that leads to the garage.

I sigh. "Guess I'll let myself out."

Something has to be done about Amelia. I'm not letting her hurt Adam in any way.

8

Adam

It's been three days since Kayla turned down my nonproposal. I'm not sure how things got so twisted around, but the end result is I'm off the hook for her sex goal. Permanently.

Yet I can't stop thinking about her.

The way her eyes flashed when she said Amelia didn't deserve me was hot. But not just that, she clearly cares about me. I heard it in the fierceness of her voice, felt it on a gut level. Why do I keep pushing her away? Who am I trying to protect here, her or me? Am I really going to hold back because of what Amelia did to me? Seeing them together, there's just no comparison. Kayla is ten times the woman Amelia is.

I grab my keys and head out the front door, adrenaline racing through me. I'm going to The Horseman Inn. It's Thursday night, which means it's ladies' night, and if there's a bunch of guys who show up, then I'll just step in as Kayla's fake fiancé. It's as good an excuse as any. She always goes to ladies' night to hang with Sydney, Jenna, and Audrey.

Hell. I miss her. *Three days.*

I miss her beaming smile that lights up her big brown eyes. I miss her delighted laugh, her direct way of speaking, the way she smells like flowers. And, yes, I miss the way she constantly compliments me. Wyatt also compliments my work, but it's not the same. Kayla makes me feel like a rock star.

I park and tell myself I'm not here for selfish reasons. I'm not searching for compliments or vying for her attention. I'm just going to get some dinner at the bar and watch the Yankees game. If she needs protection from the wrong guy, I'll step up. That's all. She doesn't need to know how much I missed her. She'll think I'm desperately following up after she turned down my proposal, even though I never actually proposed. I let it stand to get me off the hook, and suddenly I want back on the hook.

This is so messed up.

A few moments later, I step into the bar area, my gaze zeroing in on Kayla's bright smile right away. She's leaning toward Jenna, telling her something.

I casually make my way around the end of the bar, where Drew has a corner table in the back, away from the chattering ladies. He has a beer in front of him, his gaze on the TV above the bar.

I take the seat across from him. "Noisy in here."

He grunts. If Kayla thought *I* was quiet, Drew is practically mute.

I glance over at the TV, tied score Yanks versus Red Sox. Should be an interesting game. I casually shift to see what Kayla's up to. She's on the end barstool closest to me, which makes her approachable to any guy. Jenna's on her other side and then Sydney. Wyatt's behind the bar, along with the bartender Betsy. A bunch of other women I recognize are here too, locals, many of them married, just out for a night with friends. Only a couple of guys are at the other side of the bar, both teachers, in their thirties. They're talking to each other and regularly checking out the women.

Thirties is too old for Kayla. She's only twenty-five. I conveniently forget the fact that she thought I was a suitable candidate at thirty.

"I'm getting a beer and some wings," I tell Drew. "Want something?"

"I'll take some…" He trails off, his gaze suddenly intensely fixated on the other side of the room. I turn, spotting Audrey with a guy I've never seen before. He's tall and thin, his light brown hair slicked back, and he's wearing a red tie with his white dress shirt, gray trousers, and dress shoes. A little dressy for this place. They take a seat in the back dining room.

I turn back to Drew. "What do you want?"

He stands, his gaze locked on Audrey and her date. "I'll get it."

Audrey waves over to the bar area. Drew holds a hand up in acknowledgment before realizing she's waving at her friends. They give her a thumbs-up on her date. Drew drops his hand and abruptly takes his seat, staring resolutely at the TV.

"I'll get enough wings to share," I say and head over to the bar to order right by Kayla. "Hey."

She doesn't notice me, deep in conversation with Jenna and Sydney. I hear eLoveMatch and compatibility profile. That's more of a relationship app. Kayla isn't considering that, is she? I thought she just wanted a hookup. My gut churns. Now that Kayla let me off the hook, it makes me crazy thinking of her on the prowl. She should be looking for a relationship. That's what will ultimately make her happy.

I order a beer and a large order of wings. Then I eavesdrop shamelessly. The women are whispering about Audrey's date and the results of the compatibility profile. It must be Audrey on eLoveMatch. Some of the tension leaves my shoulders, which makes no sense. I should want Kayla to go in that direction.

Kayla suddenly turns, noticing me on her other side. "I thought I recognized that woodsy cologne. How're you doing, Adam?"

"I'm good, thanks."

Jenna smiles at me, a knowing look in her eyes. "Hey, Adam." *Did Kayla tell her I proposed? Or that she asked me to help her out with losing her virginity?*

The tips of my ears burn. "Hey."

Sydney waves at me, also with a knowing look in her eyes. *What did Kayla say?*

"So Audrey's doing eLoveMatch?" I ask Kayla.

"Yes. And she's really making an effort to meet the right guy. Lots of first dates." She lowers her voice. "She brings them here so one of us can check him out. We give her the thumbs up or down."

"Just from the way the guy looks?"

"That and the way he handles himself. Does he smile, seem attentive, hold her chair out for her, that kind of thing. Audrey wants a man who enjoys reading and has fine manners. I don't think that's such a difficult wish list, do you?"

"Uh, I don't know." I can't think of anyone who meets that criteria.

"There's plenty of literate men who have manners," she says. "I used to meet guys like that in school all the time."

That's not me. She wanted *me*. "But that's not what's on your wish list."

She raises her glass of wine, hiding a smile. "Not anymore."

Goose bumps rise on my arms and not the good kind. *Please tell me she hasn't already moved on. It's only been three days.*

The bartender, Betsy, delivers my beer and wings. She winks. "Here you go. Careful, hot stuff."

"Thanks." I pull some cash from my wallet, my excuse to talk to Kayla rapidly vanishing. I pay and turn to Kayla. "What've you been up to?"

She waves airily. "This and that. Had a good interview in the city yesterday."

I study her for a long moment. She looks the same as always, an angelic quality to her. Sweet and wholesome. There's no way she carried through with her plan so quickly. At the very least, she'd arrange for it on the weekend. Unless she's working this weekend.

"Good," I say. "What're you doing this weekend?"

"I'm working. Sydney needs me on for the busiest times Friday and Saturday nights."

"What about Sunday night?"

"She might be busy," Jenna singsongs.

Kayla turns to her and laughs.

My gut churns. Jenna's encouraging her. Kayla must've confided in Jenna about her so-called problem. I wish Kayla weren't in such a hurry. This could end very badly for her.

I walk back to my table and set the wings down in the center. Then I chug half my beer.

"Slow down," Drew says.

"Shut up."

"Say again," he says quietly.

I still. Drew's three years older than me, and he'd never kick my ass, but there's something about his quiet tone that's just this short of lethal. You'd have to be an idiot to ignore it. "Rough day. Not you."

He takes a wing, eyes me for a long moment, and returns his gaze to the game.

I relax. It's not like I can talk about the Kayla problem when she's sitting right there. Though I'm sure if I told Drew about it, he'd say if I'm not doing anything about it, then it's not my business. But he doesn't understand our friendship. Friends don't let friends have bad first sexual experiences. God, I wish I could stop obsessing about this.

I dig into the wings and watch the game, my ears perked for any conversational tidbit from Kayla's direction that seems relevant. I'm just looking out for her.

Mostly she's talking to her friends, something about the Fierce trilogy movies. I need to stop spying on her. She's fine. Movies can't hurt her.

"Thank you!" she calls, holding up her wineglass to the two guys in their thirties at the end of the bar. They're teachers from the high school.

Jenna gestures them over.

No.

Next thing I know, the guys are blocking my view, one standing next to Kayla, the other next to Jenna.

A fist slams on the table, startling me. I look up, and Drew gives me a head shake.

"What?" I ask with a scowl.

He leans across the table. "If you're not going to make your move, you need to clear out. You're way too obvious staring over there."

I knew he'd take that stance. He's definite, always yes or no, in or out. I don't think he's ever been unclear about anything in his life. "I'm not staring."

He gives me his dead-eye look of disbelief.

I'm about to protest that Kayla is my friend, but even I don't believe that anymore. She couldn't get what she wanted from me, so she's moved on. Dammit. I can't stand to watch a guy hitting on her. "I'm going home."

Drew lifts a hand. "Probably for the best."

His know-it-all big-brother manner irks me. I lean across the table. "You're not much better, spying on Audrey. Why don't you make a move?"

His expression shutters closed. "Audrey's confused. She doesn't know what she wants."

"So you're not even going to try?"

"I was her schoolgirl crush. Nothing real." His eyes trail over to her table and then back to the game, his jaw tight.

"Right."

I stand, take one last look at Kayla talking enthusiastically to high school math teacher Steve Zimmer, and make my way out.

Fuck it.

I do an about-face, come up behind her, and tip her head back, leaning over her. "Hello, my sweet fiancée."

She smiles. "Hello. I thought you left."

"Couldn't bear to leave you so soon."

I gesture for Steve to step out of the way. He grumbles and backs away. I take his spot and grin at her.

"You're bad," she whispers.

"What? I was helping you out. What are friends for?"

"They're not for what I hoped they were for. At least you aren't."

I tuck a lock of hair behind her ear. "I've been thinking about that."

Her cheeks flush pink, her brown eyes bright and eager. "You have?"

"Hello, what's going on here?" a male voice barks from behind the bar.

I turn to face Wyatt. "Hey, Wyatt, how was your honeymoon?"

"Great, thanks," he snaps, his eyes shifting from me to Kayla and back to me. "What did I miss?"

"We're engaged," Kayla says, holding up her ring with a laugh.

Wyatt grabs her hand and examines the ring. He whispers fiercely, "This is Paige's ring. What kind of game are you playing? And whose idea was it?"

"Relax." Kayla stands and glances around the bar before gesturing him closer. He leans across the bar. She whispers to him about my ex and pretending to be engaged to keep her away.

Wyatt straightens. "That's it? Nothing else going on?"

"Nothing else," I reassure him. *At least not yet.*

Kayla turns to me, a warm look in her eyes. "Just good friends."

The blood rushes through my veins. There's still a chance for us. I mean, to help her out.

Wait, did I just say *us*?

Kayla

Wyatt invited me to Sunday brunch at the 1950s diner in town. He knows how much I love waffles. It's a cute little place behind the gas station. Across the street is a shopping plaza with a drugstore, bagel place, pizzeria, and Chinese restaurant. It's been a while since I've seen Wyatt just the two of us. It's nice that he made time for me.

He's sporting a neatly trimmed dark beard and a deep tan from his recent honeymoon. We have similar thick dark brown hair and brown eyes. He does his usual checking in on my job search and what kind of job tasks I'm most excited to dig into at work. He's of the opinion that you need to be jazzed about something at work to really make a difference. I do love math. Dad was a math professor at Princeton University, and I have a natural aptitude for it. I ask Wyatt all about his honeymoon in Bora Bora, and he's happy to share tons of pictures.

Finally, just as I finish my Belgian waffle with strawberries and whipped cream, Wyatt pins me with a hard look. "Whose idea was the fake engagement?"

"I guess it was my idea first. I asked Adam to pretend to be my fiancé at a party at my professor's house because I knew Rob would be there."

"Rob the asshole who left you at the altar."

"Yes, but now I'm glad that happened. It was a bad idea. He only rushed me to elope because of my rule to wait for marriage. It seems pretty obvious now."

"I'm glad it didn't happen either, even though I hated seeing you suffer."

I reach across the table and give his arm a squeeze. "Thanks. I owe you for taking me in and helping me put myself together again."

"Anytime. I mean that. Even now that I'm married, if you need a safe place to land, the door is always open."

My throat tightens over a lump of emotion. "Thanks, Wyatt. You're the best brother in the world."

He inclines his head. "So you invited Adam to play fiancé at a party, and then you decided to keep playing the game when his ex came back to town. Is that how it went?"

"Basically."

"And how long will you be playing the fiancée game?"

"Just for the summer."

He slices a hand through the air. "A whole summer?"

"Yeah, it's not that big a deal."

He presses his lips together. "Kayla."

"What? It's fine."

"You can only play a game like this for so long before one of you starts believing it. And that's probably going to be you.

I don't want to see you get hurt again. This is not a good idea. For your own sake, you should just stop."

"But Amelia's still in town. She regularly pops up at his place. It's important that she knows we're together and serious about each other."

He taps the table. "Let's cut to the chase. Do you see yourself being with him as an actual couple?"

I look out the window. I do have feelings for Adam, but I can't help but think he's not capable of more than casual yet, especially with the reminder of Amelia in town. "I don't know."

"That means yes. I know you, Kayla, you're soft-hearted. This is why you have to protect yourself. Let him deal with his ex on his own."

I let out a breath. "We're just friends. You don't have to worry about it, okay?"

Unfortunately, that's the depressing truth. Sure, we've texted a bit over this weekend, but I had to work Friday and Saturday. Today's Sunday, and Adam didn't invite me to do anything. Maybe he's happy thinking I turned down his proposal, and now we're just going back to the way things were. Boy, that really backfired.

The waitress stops by, and Wyatt orders a coffee. I stick with water since I had coffee earlier.

My phone chimes with a text, and I pull it from my purse. "Just need to check in case it's work."

Adam: *What're you doing today?*

My heart thumps harder.

Me: *I'm having brunch with Wyatt, but I'm free after.*

Adam: *Is he mad about the fake-engagement stuff?*

Me: *He's just looking out for me like usual.*

"Do they need you at work?" Wyatt asks.

Adam: *Tell him we're just friends.*

My heart sinks, even though that's exactly what I told Wyatt already. I look up at him. "No, it's not work."

"Who is it? You looked happy and then sad."

He really does know me well. He's been looking out for me through life's up and downs since I was seven years old.

Except now I'm a full-grown woman capable of making my own mistakes and good choices alike. I'm not sure which Adam is; all I know is that I want to find out.

I text back. *I'll call you after this.*

I tuck my phone back in my purse. "It's Adam. I think he needs me to play fiancée later."

Wyatt leans back and shakes his head at me. "Not smart. Use your brain."

I sigh. "I'm an adult now. I can handle whatever life throws at me."

"That doesn't mean you do something you know isn't good for you."

I meet his eyes and say in a firm voice, "We're friends, and if it leads to something more, well, I'm okay with that."

His light brown eyes go soft. "I know you are, runt. It's him I'm worried about."

9

I return home to put on a new outfit—red halter top, white skirt, and heeled sandals with leather ties that wrap around my ankles. I need to shed my wholesome vibe, and this is the sexiest outfit I own. Maybe I should pick up stilettos.

With fresh determination, I head over to my Jeep and climb inside. I check my look in the mirror and fluff my hair out, attempting a sexy tousled look.

I pull out of the lot and drive around the other side of the lake and down a long street toward Adam's place. I didn't call. I'm just going to show up.

Once there, I look up at his well-kept two-story colonial house. This time I'm putting it all on the line. I'm going to share my growing feelings, let him know this isn't just about sex, and it's time we give us a chance.

Oof, oof, oof. Tank barks at me through the living room window, his big adorable head in front of the sheer curtain. Adam pulls back the curtain and looks at me too. His dark good looks in a T-shirt and jeans send a jolt through my system.

I wave, frozen in place. A small voice in my head says I should leave, and a louder voice says to shut up. Suddenly it feels like a lot more is on the line than just my V-card. My heart is thundering, as though it knows I'm about to crack open the tidy safe cage I've kept it hidden in.

The front door opens a moment later. Adam takes a slow perusal from my tousled hair to my halter top, skirt, all the way to my toes. He slowly lifts his head, his eyes smoldering into mine.

My breath hitches. "I came here today—"

"I know why you're here." And then he yanks me inside, hauling me against his body, his mouth crashing down over mine. Heat flashes through me, and an ache low in my belly says this is *exactly* what I need. I'm vaguely aware of the door shutting behind me. The sensations flooding my brain leave me in a rare state of complete static shutdown.

His mouth gentles, sliding kiss after kiss, his warm hand cradling my cheek. *So good.* My nipples go tight and hard, sensation racing over my skin. I wrap my arms around his neck and press close. His hands slide down my sides and over the curve of my hips and back up. His kisses are long and deep, and my body softens weakly against him.

His hand slides to my bottom, holding me to him. His scent, his taste, the deep kisses all combine to lull me into a mindless rhythm, my hips arching, seeking more.

He shifts to trail his mouth along my neck.

I catch my breath, a niggling thought entering my mind. "I'm not the wholesome girl you marry someday. I'm the kind you fuck right now."

He mutters a curse, his gaze smoldering into mine as he unties my halter top. I think he got the message. It's the kind of top you don't need a bra with, and a moment later I'm completely exposed.

His lips meet mine as he caresses my breasts, his thumbs brushing back and forth across my hard nipples. Lost in sensation, my fingers clutch his shirt. A throbbing sensation I'm only fleetingly familiar with makes me dizzy with lust. He bends, his tongue tracing my nipple before he draws it into his mouth. Each tug brings an insistent throb, a pulse of raw need. I run my fingers through his hair, my knees getting weaker by the moment. By the time he switches to the other breast, I'm soaked with desire.

"I want everything," I say. "Now. Right now."

His mouth covers mine, silencing me with more deep kisses. I pull his shirt and then slide my hands under it. His skin is heated, the hard muscular planes of his back exciting me. He hitches up my skirt, pushes my panties out of the way, and traces me intimately.

I gasp, the sensation new for me.

He lifts his head, his eyes locking on mine for a long moment. His hand cups me but stops moving.

I grab his arm. "Don't stop."

He searches my expression before claiming my mouth again. His fingers stroke the shape of me, tracing up and down, sending a riot of sensation through me. I clutch his muscular arm as it flexes while he directs the action at pleasure central. My knees give out, but he's got me, one arm banded tightly around my waist.

And then he stops, no action down below. I tear my mouth away to protest. He backs me up, guiding me toward the sofa.

He barks out an order for Tank to go to his bed.

I smile as Tank obeys, flopping down on his bed. "If you order me to bed, I'll go."

He gives me a little push, and I land on the sofa. "Here will do."

I peel off my halter top, which was just hanging around my waist, and toss it to the side. I'm pretty confident this is the right time to strip. I reach for his shirt, but he pushes me back, goes to his knees, and runs his hands along the outside of my bare thighs. He pushes my skirt up out of the way, and then his fingers hook in the thin waistband of my panties, and he slides them off.

"Spread your legs," Adam murmurs.

I comply, shivering in anticipation. He grabs my hips and pulls me forward. And then he tastes me. My hips jerk, the intimate sensation shockingly intense.

"Relax," he murmurs, looking up at me from between my

legs. "I'll take good care of you."

I let out a shaky breath. "I know. It's just—" I suck in air as his mouth returns, kissing and tasting me. He's gentle, letting me get used to him. A warm tingly glow flows over my entire body, and I relax.

I close my eyes, floating in sensation. His finger traces my opening, and I tense, anticipating pain when he enters me. This is why I never let it get this far. I never trusted the guy to hold back when I needed it. But he doesn't do anything more, merely tracing me, shifting away and back, away and back, his mouth working magic.

I open my eyes, his dark head between my legs sending another riot of sensation through me. His mouth becomes more insistent, drawing me toward something darker, deeper. Everything inside me coils tight. I'm panting, my hips rocking mindlessly, fever hot. The orgasm rips through me like a tidal wave, threatening to take me under. I buck helplessly under him, shuddering with the rush of pleasure.

"Omigod, that was…" I gasp and let out a soft keening cry, my head tipping back as he keeps it going, drawing more pleasure out of me, wave after wave until I go limp. I try to catch my breath. I've definitely been missing out on this before. I never knew it could be like that. My own efforts pale in comparison.

I let him dress me, too spent to move. He slides my panties back in place, fixes my skirt, and then pulls my halter top back over my head, lifting me to straighten it and tying the knot behind my neck.

I'm still tingling all over—my lips, my cheeks, my nipples, my sex. We should go to his bed. I can't seem to speak. I feel like I'm drugged.

He pulls me off the sofa, wrapping his arms around me. I rest my head against his chest as his hands glide up and down my back, over my bottom, my hips.

I lift my head, a soft smile on my lips. I feel so good right now. "Adam."

"Yeah."

"I want to—"

He silences me with a kiss, and I taste myself. It only excites me more. This sexy man knows me intimately. I reach for the button on his jeans. He grabs my wrists, holding them in a firm grip at my sides while his mouth plunders mine. A sharp rush of desire makes me suddenly frantic for more. I plaster myself against him, arching forward, aching for him to take.

He breaks the kiss. "How do you feel?"

"Amazing! Now—"

He turns me toward the door. "I'll see you next weekend."

My jaw drops. I turn back to face him. "You're making me wait a week?"

"I'm working weekdays, and you work Friday and Saturday night. Sunday, I'll take you in a rowboat like you wanted."

I frown. I did think that was a romantic idea before, but he just opened up a whole new world for me. And even though I feel exhilarated, there's still an ache deep inside that needs to be filled. "Adam, only you will do."

He groans, framing my face with his hands. "Please do this for me. Go home. I'll see you Sunday."

I lick my lips. "What about you? I should reciprocate, don't you think?" I felt his hard desire.

"I'll take care of that after you go."

"Can I—"

His mouth covers mine, and then he's backing me up, his kisses insistent, one after the other. Dizzying lust has me off balance. He spins me suddenly and gives my bottom a pat.

Then he pushes me out the front door.

I stand there for a moment, blinking against the sun, a little disoriented. A car drives by; birds chirp; a child yells in the distance. The world's still spinning around while mine went right off its axis.

I texted Adam to find out what he's working on this week, and it turns out it's a local job. That means he'll be home a little after five. I calculated commute time from anywhere in town, allowing for the possibility that he'd want to shower and change, and here I am with Chinese food for our dinner together. It's the day after he gave me the best orgasm of my life, of which there's only been the self-given variety. I've definitely been missing out.

And we did *not* agree on waiting a week to see each other. He said it; I protested. Besides, friends can hang out whenever they want, especially when one friend has just experienced the orgasm of her life from the other friend. That's my story and I'm sticking to it.

Did I wear another skirt to give him easy access? Damn right I did. Today's outfit is a yellow blouse with cap sleeves and a blue ruffled skirt. I don't know if it screams sexy, but it does say *go ahead and lift this bit of fluffy skirt out of the way and have your wicked way with me*.

I ring the bell, and Tank sets off the alarm. *Oof, oof, oof.* I wiggle my fingers at him as he sticks his head under the curtain to look at me.

The front door opens to Adam, dark hair still damp from the shower, shirtless and barefoot in jeans. My lips part, my pulse thrumming through my veins. I've never seen him shirtless, and he's *amazing*. Wide rounded shoulders, defined pecs and abs, a smattering of chest hair leading straight down to the fly in his jeans. I need to peel those jeans off and—

"Whatcha doing here, Kayla?"

I meet his eyes, warm on mine. He's happy to see me. "I brought dinner." I hold up the bag. "Chinese food."

He gestures me in. "This is a surprise. I'll go get a shirt."

"I think you look fantastic just as you are," I say in a breathy voice.

One corner of his mouth lifts before he turns and goes upstairs. I appreciate the rear view immensely.

After he disappears to his bedroom, I find my way to the kitchen just off the dining room. Tank shuffles after me, hoping for some food. I poke around in cabinets until I find what I need to set the table. Then I pull all the take-out containers out of the bag and set them on the table too.

He returns. "This is better than what I was going to have. Frozen dinner in front of the TV. Thanks."

I smile. "No problem. I didn't know what you'd like, so I got five different things."

He closes the distance, standing close. My heart kicks up an excited beat. He smells fresh and clean. I want to bury my face in his neck and just breathe. He holds my chin, tipping my face to his, and kisses me. I nearly sigh.

"Sweet of you," he says. "I'm not picky." He moves to the cabinet, getting us two glasses and filling them with water.

I take a seat and he sits across from me.

I wait until he's served himself before clearing the air. "I hope you're okay with me just showing up here. It's just that I had a really, *really* good time yesterday—" I flush hot at the memory "—and I always like spending time with you anyway because you're you, and I—"

"Kayla, it's okay. We don't have to wait a week to see each other. I was just trying not to ravish you in the living room."

"But I want you to ravish me in the living room and other places too. Anywhere is fine by me."

He stares at me for a heated moment. And then he slowly stands, intent in his eyes. A shiver of excitement races down my spine. He stalks around the table toward me. I'm half hopeful and half afraid he's about to kick me out. He's been very up and down about the sex part.

I stand, considering throwing myself in his arms in a desperate shortcut to seduction. But then I don't need to. He pulls me against him, his mouth claiming mine. This time I don't hesitate, roaming my hands all over him, dying to feel skin on skin. I manage to get his shirt loose from his jeans, and my hands shoot up, stroking his back and his heated chest. His kisses become more aggressive, his fingers tangling in my hair. He's moving me, backing me up. My back hits cool wall.

He shifts, his mouth trailing over my jaw, nipping and tasting, jolting and soothing me. I'm breathless. He moves to my throat, my collarbone, my breasts through the thin blouse, sucking my hard nipple, flooding me with pleasure. I want to reciprocate this time, my hand going to his waistband, tracing inside the edge, but then I stop, suddenly anxious that I'll do it wrong. My inexperience embarrasses me.

"Tell me what to do," I say.

He straightens, his teeth tugging my earlobe. "You don't have to do anything," he whispers. "Let me."

Before I can protest, his mouth's on mine, his fingers making quick work of my blouse. He breaks the kiss, slides my bra straps over my shoulders, and undoes the clasp.

"You too," I say, yanking his shirt up. He lets me take it off, and I'm high on victory. I throw my arms around his neck, the sensation of skin on skin so delicious I rub myself shamelessly against him.

His big hand cups my jaw, his eyes meeting mine for a charged moment before he kisses me again and again. There's never been a kisser in the world as good as this man. My breath is ragged by the time he lifts his head.

He drops to his knees, and I suck in air, remembering yesterday when he went to his knees. He slides my panties off and then rises in one smooth motion, his fingers gripping my hair as he kisses me aggressively, pressing my mouth open, tasting deep. My entire body goes heavy with desire, my hands clutching his shoulders for support in the storm of sensation.

His hand slides under my skirt, and he groans when he feels how wet I am. He strokes gently up and down, and I arch my hips for more. His thumb skates over pleasure central, and I suddenly want to climb him, wrap my legs around him, and know what it's like to be filled. I ache deeply for him. I lift my leg, wrapping it high around his hip, hoping he'll get the message.

He breaks the kiss to whisper in my ear, his thumb still working magic. "Relax, this is for you."

"I like it," I gasp out. "But…" His thumb applies more pressure. "Adam," I finish weakly, setting my leg down.

He cups the back of my neck, kissing me again, deep and thorough as his thumb works me. Sensations riot through me, building faster and faster. My body bows, and then I break, his mouth swallowing my soft cries. His thumb gentles, extending the pleasure in a long, rolling wave. I whimper and go limp, leaning back against the wall, panting.

He kisses me gently and pulls back, watching me intently.

I stroke his scruffy cheek. "Please don't kick me out."

He folds me into his arms. "I'm not going to kick you out. We didn't even eat this awesome dinner you brought."

I look over his shoulder. "Uh-oh. Tank ate your dinner." Fortunately, I hadn't served myself yet.

He turns to find his plate licked clean. "Tank! Outside."

Tank hangs his head like this is the worst punishment in the world. He prefers to stay inside. I try not to laugh. Adam puts him in the fenced-in backyard and orders him to do his business.

I stick my panties in my purse so Adam will know I'm available after dinner too. I take a seat at the table, helping myself to dinner and reheating it in the microwave.

Adam returns with a not-at-all contrite Tank. I wait for Adam to get himself a clean plate and more food, taking a minute to heat it up. Once he settles at the table, Tank lies at his feet, looking hopeful for scraps now that he knows how good the food is.

I smile at Adam. "I left my panties off."

He drops his fork with a clatter. "Kayla." His voice is hoarse, his eyes closed with a pained expression. "What're you doing to me?"

"I've got plans that involve full reciprocation," I inform him.

And then I pop up and quickly drop sideways into his lap so he knows I mean it.

His hand cradles my jaw, his forehead pressing against mine for a moment. We share a breath and then another, and then his lips meet mine.

More drugging kisses. *I'm irresistible as a sex partner.*

His hand's up my shirt, caressing my breast. *What a relief to leave my wholesome future-wife image behind!*

I gasp as his other hand pushes my skirt out of the way. *Mmm, yes, yes, YES!*

10

Adam

I'm playing with fire and I know it. Yet I can't seem to help myself. No man could. Kayla stopped by every night this week to have dinner with me, and she's so sexy, so eager to press herself against me, I give her an orgasm for her efforts. I haven't let her return the favor because I know the moment I'm naked, I'm not going to be thinking straight anymore. It claws at me, this need. But she's waited all this time for sex with marriage, and I can't help but think she's the kind of woman who needs that, whether or not she realizes it in her currently horny state.

I care too much about her to let her have regrets.

And some part of me knows, if I cross that line, there's no going back. I'll be lost in her, and then she'll leave. I can't risk it.

Casual. We both agreed it's casual.

It's Friday night, which means she has to work, so I stop by The Horseman Inn just to say hi. Like I said, casual. I walk into the front dining room just as she turns with used dinner plates balanced in her arms. One plate goes flying, and the ceramic shatters on the hardwood floor.

She stares at it. "Oops! Sorry!"

The customers at her table laugh good-naturedly. "That's

okay, honey," the middle-aged woman says. "Happens to the best of us."

Her husband agrees, even standing to help.

Kayla holds him back with a palm. "It's okay. I'll get this cleaned up in a minute." Her eyes fly to mine. "Adam."

The blood rushes through my veins. I want to take her to a dark corner and press my mouth on hers, kiss her until she melts against me, needy mewling sounds coming from the back of her throat. "Hi."

Pink tinges her cheeks. "I have to clean this up."

"Go ahead."

She rushes back to the kitchen to deposit the plates she's holding. She's wearing the uniform of a black Horseman Inn T-shirt and black pants. Nothing remotely sexy, but I can't help but watch the sway of her curvy hips as she passes.

I take a seat at the crowded bar, mostly middle-aged women who are alternating knitting and drinking. Probably they hung around after Friday trivia night. Sydney mentioned she has knitting club regulars then. I order a seltzer and pot stickers. The menu's become much more interesting with the new chef. I respect his work, even though Sydney says he's a shameless flirt, which doesn't make me feel great about Kayla working with him.

Kayla rushes past me a few moments later with a broom and dustpan. Rushes back. Rushes out again with a mop. Rushes back. Quite a workout being a waitress. At least for her it is.

My gaze tracks to her again and again as she smiles and chats with customers, occasionally dropping silverware or a straw. She's a people person, unlike me. I like people in small quantities. Except her I can't seem to get enough of. That's okay, it won't get too far. She's been going on plenty of interviews. Any day now she'll split for her new adventure. I'll just be a hazy memory of one summer. A summer fling, that's what this is. One that involves her pleasure and my aching need. It's torture, sweet torture, but I want to give this to her. She's new to sex, all of it. I was the first man to touch her, taste her, feel her come apart. And that's not a small thing. She trusts me, and I won't betray that trust by disappointing her with no real intention of a committed relationship. I don't know why I'm so twisted up about this. I'm avoiding relationships, and she's leaving. It should be perfect.

I finish my dinner, no real excuse to hang around anymore. I'm tired from hard labor at work today, hauling large beams of wood for an addition.

And then she's heading straight for me, a beaming smile on her beautiful face. Warmth rushes through me, and I barely resist pulling her into my arms.

She stops short and whispers, "I have a fifteen-minute break. Come with me." She grabs my hand and gives it a tug.

I know I shouldn't. She's just going to want more of what we do every time we see each other. It's getting harder and harder—exactly the problem.

"Let's go for a walk around the lake," I say.

"We'll go out the back," she says.

I follow her through the kitchen.

Spencer, the new chef, grins at her. "Kayla, woman, you'd better not drop this fine T-bone I'm serving tonight." He's too good looking with his dark hair, blue eyes, and beard. I could grow a beard if I felt like moving beyond scruff. And I didn't miss the innuendo in his flirty comment. *Serving a T-bone. He wants to bone her.*

Kayla laughs. "I swear I won't!" She didn't catch the innuendo. Still an innocent to lewd guys.

I narrow my eyes at him.

"Adam," he says with a nod.

"Spencer," I bite out.

Kayla looks between us and then forges ahead through the door that leads to the back stairs up to her apartment.

"I thought we were going for a walk," I say, following her fine ass upstairs.

"You're walking, aren't you?"

She lets me into her apartment, which is miniscule. I've been up here many times before she moved in. What would be a living room is used as storage for the restaurant. She only has a bedroom and a bathroom. She has to use the kitchen downstairs.

She slips into her bedroom.

I tell myself to be cool. Fifteen minutes is not much time. Maybe we should talk like we're having an actual date instead of this smokescreen we put up when all we really want to do is rip each other's clothes off.

Her T-shirt goes flying into the hallway a few feet ahead of me. Then a black lacy bra.

I swallow hard.

She follows a moment later, stepping into my personal space, bold as you please. "Hello, stranger."

I grab her, my mouth on hers, my hands stroking all over her curvy body. I slide a hand to her ass and then between her legs, her moan vibrating against my mouth. *I need, I need.*

I can't keep doing this.

I can't stop doing this.

Within minutes, she's writhing against me, naked, my fingers expertly working her. I send her over, thrilling in her soft cries, the way her body shudders against mine.

We're still standing. One of us naked.

I ache fiercely. I don't know how much longer I can hold out.

"Adam," she says, pulling at the button on my jeans, "please let me."

I shift away, gather up her clothes, and hand them to her. "You'd better get back to work."

"You're still holding me to a month of waiting?" she asks incredulously.

I completely forgot about my ridiculous schedule for seduction. "Yeah."

She sighs and pulls her bra on. Her chest is still flushed pink from her orgasm. I know what she likes now, how to get her there fast or slow. Tonight was fast because of the time limit.

I turn away, done torturing myself with her sexy body.

And then she surprises me, wrapping her arms around me from behind in a hug. "I'm going to wear you down."

It wouldn't take much.

Adam

I decided Kayla and I need more time in public together to limit the temptation, so I invited her to go fishing today. I park in the lot of The Horseman Inn and text her. It's early Sunday morning, before sunrise, which is the best time to get out on the lake. The fish are biting at dawn.

A few minutes later, she appears, her hair up in a ponytail, wearing a T-shirt that looks strangely boxy on her curvy figure, jeans, and mismatched shoes. She squints at me and then makes her way to the car.

I get out to meet her. She's wearing a black sandal with a beige one, and her shirt is on backwards and inside out. "Morning. Do you want to go put on matching sandals?"

She looks down and back up at me. "I'm still a zombie. Why do we have to fish at dawn, again?"

"Because that's when the fish are biting."

She waves at her feet. "I'm comfortable." She wiggles her shoulders. "My shirt must've shrunk in the wash."

"It's backwards."

"What?" She looks down at the tag. "Oh, it's inside out."

"Yeah, inside out and back—Kayla!" I spread my arms wide, blocking her from any Peeping Toms. She just whipped her shirt off. No bra. *Not looking, not looking.*

"There," she says. "Let's go."

I glance down. Shirt on right. Ponytail askew. Good enough.

A short while later, we're on the lake in my rowboat, Kayla yawning mightily. "I worked until midnight," she says. "I only got five hours of sleep."

"It'll be worth it. Have you ever watched the sunrise?"

"No."

"It's beautiful. Plus you can catch your first fish." She's holding the rod I borrowed from my neighbor Levi.

"Are you sure these fake worms fool the fish?" she asks.

"Yes."

"Well, so far, no fish have fallen for your trick."

"Just wait and see."

She gets quiet, which is good. You want to be still and quiet when you're fishing. I relax as the sun's first rays show through the leafy green canopy surrounding us. Nothing better than being out on the water on a warm summer day.

I glance at Kayla to see how she's enjoying it. Her head is lolling forward. I nudge her foot with my foot, and she startles awake. "Did I miss it?" She looks around. "Oh, there it is. Sunrise. I'm good now. Can we—ah! Adam!" She tightens her grip on the rod. "I caught something! It must be huge. It's pulling hard. What do I do?"

"Reel it in. Use the—"

She flings her rod up and over into the boat, a small trout wriggling on the end. "Grab it! I don't want it to touch me!"

"It's catch and release. You have to throw it back."

She swings the rod wildly. "Release it!"

"Stop swinging the rod. Grab the fish, take it off the hook, and throw it back."

"You grab the fish!"

"I can't because you keep moving it around."

She stills and stares at it with huge eyes, where it's flopping in the bottom of the boat. "Adam!"

"It's going to die if you don't throw it back."

She grabs it and flings it overboard. I'll make a fisherwoman of her yet.

Then she holds her palms up to me, panting. "I need hand sanitizer."

Or not.

≈

Kayla

I fear I made a bad impression on Adam last Sunday when we went fishing, and it's important that we connect doing his favorite activity outside of work. After all, he's always happy to do what I want. So here I am for fishing date number two. This time I've set myself up for success.

First, it's eleven a.m., a reasonable hour for two people to go out on the lake. I'm not convinced you need to go fishing at dawn. Adam admitted he's never tried fishing late in the morning since his dad taught him you have to fish at sunrise. We can both learn something new today. Second, I prepared by going to Mike's Bait and Tackle shop, a cute place that looks like it hasn't changed since it opened in 1969. Mike was very happy to have me as a customer.

Adam just texted me that he's here. I bound down the steps and push open the door of the restaurant to a beautiful sunny June day. I'm all caffeinated, showered, and wearing a cute pink V-neck T-shirt with denim shorts and matching beige sandals. I had to make up for last week's disheveled appearance. Fortunately, it was mostly dim and dark in the wee hours last Sunday, so I don't think he got a good look at me then.

"Morning!" I call.

Adam's leaning against his car, his long jeans-clad legs crossed at the ankle. "Afternoon."

"No, it's before noon." I walk over and hold up my white bakery bag. "I brought breakfast."

He opens the bag. "Cupcakes for breakfast?"

"They're chocolate muffins."

He arches a brow. "Looks like chocolate cupcakes."

"Muffins are healthy for you."

"If you say so."

He opens the passenger-side door for me and shuts it behind me. Lately, Adam's been doing more of these polite gestures like we're a couple. I know we said it's casual, but it's starting to feel different to me.

I wait until we're out on the lake in his cute white rowboat with navy trim to give him his surprise. He's leaning back in a Yankees cap with sunglasses, looking relaxed.

I open my large white Kate Spade hobo bag, a splurge when I earned my master's degree, and pull out my find. "I went to Mike's Bait and Tackle shop and got you this." I hand over a red cap that has two fish facing each other with the shop's name. Then I put my matching one on.

He stares at it. "Thanks."

I hold my palm out. "Here, I'll put your Yankees cap in my purse. Go ahead and put it on."

He inspects the inside of it before switching the new cap for the old one. I tuck his hat in my purse and smile.

"Now we look like real fishing buddies." Then I remember what we're here for. *Oops. Forgot to hold my rod during all this.* Well, it seems just fine resting on the side of the boat. No fish have bit yet, but I'm sure there will be some swimming up for lunch soon.

"Mike must've been thrilled you bought a hat," he says.

"Actually, yes, he was. Aren't they popular?"

He bites back a smile. "He got a deal ten years ago and bought three thousand of them. He still has tons left, so I'd say no, they're not popular."

"I don't see why not. We look cute. And more like official fisherpeople."

He shakes his head with a smile.

"What?"

"Nothing. Did you get any bait while you were in there?" He glances at my purse. "I'm guessing no."

"Well, I was going to. That's why I went in there, but…" I crinkle my nose. "The can of wriggling worms made me queasy, so I said no, thanks, Adam has fake worms that work just as well. Then we had a lively discussion on real versus fake worms before I finally told him that I had to go because I was meeting you. And that's when I noticed the cute hats."

"You're a force of nature."

I can't read his expression very well with the cap and sunglasses. "Is that good?"

"It's just who you are."

I quirk my lips to the side, still not sure if he's complimenting me or not. "Even you, Mr. Nature Guy, have to agree it wouldn't be sanitary to eat breakfast after touching dirty worms."

He pulls a small bottle from his back jeans pocket. "Ah, but I brought hand sanitizer this time."

I put my hand over my heart. See? He keeps doing couple-like things. "So thoughtful."

After our late breakfast, we float for a while, but there's just no action going on under the water. (Though above water, Adam kissed me several times. And, okay, I briefly stood with the intention of sitting in his lap, almost tipping us over.) In any case, not a bite on our fake worms. Other people are out on the water now, rowing canoes and rowboats. In the distance, a few people are sailing small boats.

Adam's being polite not to mention it, but after more than two hours, we haven't caught a single fish. I don't mind, they're kind of gross and slimy, but Adam enjoys the challenge, so I try to appreciate what's fun for him.

I'm not admitting defeat either because this is the time I'm willing to go fishing, and it's not so bad being out on the lake with him. Actually, it's really nice. He's very relaxed and talks more than usual, sharing about his dad and the times they went fishing together just the two of them.

I never saw myself as the kind of woman to go fishing (with no fish), but I'm happy. There's no place I'd rather be than with Adam. I may be halfway in love with him.

11

Kayla

"I'm just trying to prove a point," Jenna says, steering me to sit on the far side of the bar for our Thursday Night Wine Club. "He'll magnetize straight to you, staking his territory."

I follow her, along with Sydney. Audrey is in the back dining room on another first date from eLoveMatch. Her date seems nice—short blond hair, clean-shaven, wearing a shirt and tie. He even gave her a book, which was one of her requirements in a guy. I can't tell the title from here. We gave her the thumbs-up.

I settle at the end of the bar and take a sip of chardonnay. "Adam's not even here. And if he does show up, it's not because he's staking his territory. That's silly."

"He's like clockwork," Sydney says. "Seven thirty on the dot. Prime meat-market time."

I giggle. "I wouldn't exactly call ladies' night a meat market." It's mostly women enjoying half-price drinks with their friends just like us. A couple of guys in their thirties are here, watching the game. Drew's at his usual table in the back, eyes glued to the TV.

"He's trying to prevent another guy from asking you out," Jenna says.

My friends know we're only fake engaged. I keep telling

them we're just casual, even though part of me wishes it were more. It's not fair of me to expect more. We were both clear up front, and I understand why he doesn't want to get serious with anyone.

"He's usually hanging with Drew," I say.

"But his eyes never leave you," Sydney singsongs.

My lips curve up. "We see each other every night anyway. This is no different."

"Every night!" Jenna exclaims and then whispers, "Does that mean you finally gave up your V-card?"

Sydney leans in to hear the big news. Unfortunately, there is no news.

I paste on a smile. "No, but it's fine. We're just very, uh, close friends." *With half a benefit. Mine.* He gets me off, and then he pushes me away. Am I frustrated? Yes. But I really can't complain when he makes me feel so good.

Sydney shakes her head. "I don't get it. You fool around every night, right?"

"Shh," I say, looking around for Adam. He wouldn't appreciate me sharing the nitty-gritty. But I already told them so much there's no going back now.

"Sorry," Sydney whispers. "What's the deal?"

I gesture them both closer. "We always stop before it gets that far."

"Why?" they ask in unison.

"I think he's overprotective of me, which is nice. He's looking out for me." *Or he's just not that into me.* I don't quite get it myself.

"Just tell him it's okay to keep going," Jenna says.

"Yeah, some guys need it spelled out." Sydney's brows scrunch together. "I didn't think Adam was one of the clueless guys though. It's not like he's inexperienced. There was—"

I wave that away, not wanting to hear about all the other women Adam had sex with. "Not a big deal. I'm happy."

"But wasn't that the whole reason you crossed the line with him?" Jenna asks.

I down my wine in one long swallow. "I'm sure it'll just happen."

Jenna leans close to whisper in my ear, "Has he seen you naked? You're hot."

I blush at the compliment. Now why can't Adam say something like that? "Thanks and yes."

She straightens and signals Betsy, the bartender. "Not a good sign."

A familiar masculine voice sounds behind me. "What's not a good sign?"

I turn with a bright smile. "Adam, hi! Jenna was just saying they're running low on margarita mix. Terrible sign for ladies' night. They usually sell them by the pitcher."

He nods. "Good to see you. I'm going to watch the game with Drew."

"Sure, no problem."

He strides over to his brother.

"See?" I say. "Just normal hanging out. He's definitely not here to keep guys away."

"We'll see," Jenna says. "Just need a guy to sidle up to your side to prove it."

I roll my eyes.

Audrey squeezes in by my side. "I'm done. No more first dates. I can't take it anymore." She grabs Sydney's wine and chugs.

I look to where her date was, and he's sitting there with an older blond woman.

"What the hell?" Jenna exclaims. "Did he bring another woman on your date?"

"It's his mother," Audrey hisses. "He invited her to make sure we get along because he could never date someone Mother didn't approve of. I get that you want your family to like your significant other but on a first date?"

"That's kinda creepy," Sydney says.

"They live together," Audrey says. "He gets the downstairs, and she gets the upstairs." She shudders. "I can't even…ladies, why is this so hard? Why can't I meet a great guy who gives me all the feels?" She gestures to Sydney. "Like you did."

"Are you forgetting I used to call Wyatt Satan?" Sydney asks. "We couldn't stop fighting in the beginning."

Audrey exhales sharply. "We all knew that was just sexual tension. It was so obvious the chemistry between you two." She moans and leans over the bar top, resting her head on her forearms.

I rub her back. "I'm sure it'll happen for you when the time's right." That's what I keep hoping for with sex. I have to believe that's true or wallow in despair like Audrey here.

I glance up, catching Drew's intense stare. He's checking in on Audrey. They're friends. Kinda. I never see them talk beyond a brief hello, but that's what Audrey calls him. I think he cares for her, but doesn't know how to express it. And Audrey is prickly about him. Sydney says she suspects Audrey told him she's had a lifelong crush on him, and he didn't return the sentiment. Though at this point, with Audrey being a mature twenty-nine, I suspect it's much more than a crush. Too bad Drew's the clueless type. Maybe that runs in Sydney's family. She was clueless to how wonderful my brother Wyatt is at first. She even turned down his first proposal. Luckily, she came to her senses and realized Wyatt's a great guy.

"Yoo-hoo!" Jenna calls to a dark-haired guy wearing a backwards baseball cap down at the other end of the bar. "Can I get you a drink?"

He flashes a smile and approaches her. His friend joins him.

Audrey lifts her head and turns to me. "I'm going to end up with nine cats and a houseful of books."

"I'm sure that's not true. Besides, there's nothing wrong with a houseful of books. Maybe pare it down to two cats."

"Or a dog," Adam says, appearing by my side. "Dogs are superior companions."

Jenna pokes my shoulder in an *I told you so* gesture. She inclines her head to the two guys now standing nearby.

I study Adam with his handsome scruff in a white T-shirt

and faded jeans. His expression is the same as always, reserved. Is he really territorial about me? Is that why he came over just as Jenna called the two guys over?

Did we somehow fall into a relationship?

What is going on in his head? I used to always know. Now everything is so confusing.

He gets into a lively debate with Audrey about cats versus dogs, which is a nice distraction for her. She actually laughs.

I sigh. Jenna's wrong. He's just hanging with us. He doesn't give me any special attention whatsoever.

I have to be okay with that.

12

Kayla

It's now officially been five weeks that Adam and I have been fake engaged. That's a full week past the month he said we needed to see each other before he'd take my virginity, he still hasn't followed through, and I'm not even in complete despair. Okay, I'm a little upset, but I'm also ridiculously happy. I'm afraid I've done the unthinkable—confused casual for serious. Not that I've said anything like that. It's just when I see him, I feel lit up inside, even before he touches me. And when he smiles, those rare fleeting smiles, my heart squeezes with affection. He's just so wonderful, so thoughtful and kind. We can talk about anything and make each other laugh.

I'm more than halfway in love with him. I'm all the way.

This is not good. I don't think he's feeling the same way. If he did, he'd say something like *let's be exclusive* or ask me to be his girlfriend, something official like that. Nothing.

I'm fully aware of the irony, telling him I wanted casual and now feeling differently. But that was before we spent so much time together. I smooth out my red and white polka-dotted sundress over my knees. Adam's driving us over to Wyatt's house for a Fourth of July barbecue. Adam and I need to have a serious talk. I've been postponing it because if he doesn't return my feelings, I just know that will be the end of us. He'll cut ties, or I'll be too devastated to enjoy what we do have, and I'm just not ready to go there yet. Soon.

I sigh. We see each other every night, either at his place or at mine on my break. And it's not just us slamming together, mouths fused with burning passion. Though, there's plenty of that. We go on walks together, fishing twice, and I took him to Clover Park for the best ice cream in the world, where we hung out in the gazebo in the park, talking about anything and everything.

What have I done? Ruined our wonderful friendship by demanding he help me get rid of my virginity. All this sexy stuff has messed with my head big time.

I glance over at Adam in profile, his scruffy jaw and kissable lips so dear to me now. Actually, his jaw looks tight. "Everything okay?"

He glances at me. "Wyatt can't know we've been fooling around."

Fooling around. Definitely casual in his mind. I push down the hurt. "Like I'd tell my brother. It's none of his business."

He laughs mirthlessly. "Yeah. Let's keep it that way. You have to make it look like we're just friends. Don't do…"

"What?"

He shoots me an exasperated look. "Don't hug me and stuff."

"Friends can hug. He knows I'm an affectionate person."

"He'll take it wrong."

"Did he say something to you?" I ask, suddenly alarmed. Wyatt's always been my protector, but this is embarrassing. As far as Wyatt knows, Adam and I are good friends pretending to be engaged. Is that why Adam holds me at a distance?

He glances at me, looking guilty. "Just that…look, I didn't want to say anything, but when he saw us dancing at his wedding, he assumed you were propositioning me—"

"What!"

"Which you did later, so he wasn't far off, but at the time you were just inviting me to be your fake fiancé…" He trails off. "This is so fucked up. I don't think we should've arrived together."

I'm so irked by the men in my life trying to determine what's okay and not okay for me to do. "So I shouldn't tell him you fucked me with your mouth?"

He jerks. "Kayla."

"Or that you won't let me fuck you with my mouth? You always hold me back from true physical intimacy. We're like friends with half a benefit. It's not normal!" *And I'm still an effing virgin with way too many feelings to pretend we're just friends.*

"Nothing about this friendship has ever been normal," he returns.

I seethe in silence as he pulls up the hill to Wyatt's house. To think I have real feelings for this man who only sees me as a friend. An abnormal friendship at that.

I get out of the car the moment he parks. Then I lean back in the open passenger door. "Don't worry. I won't tell him we're abnormal friends who only let one of us get naked."

"Don't say anything at all."

I gently shut the door, so it's not obvious we're fighting, and walk to the backyard to join everyone. Wyatt's place used to be a farm. The old farmhouse with gray clapboard siding has been completely renovated with a large addition on the back. In addition to acres of flat land, rolling hills, and woodland, the property also has the unusual feature of a water tower made over to look like a lighthouse. A landlocked lighthouse. My brother appreciated the irony, which is why he bought the place.

Adam will be a few minutes, getting Tank from the back seat. Wyatt was okay with Tank having a doggie playdate with Snowball (his shih tzu) and Rexie (his pit bull). Wyatt's dogs are female, so this should be interesting for Tank.

I spot a small green canopy set up with a fan in the corner and water dishes for the dogs. Wyatt's such a good doggy dad. He's been a dad to me too since our dad died. Wyatt's six years older than me. One day he'll be a great dad to his own kids, though I know that's a few years off. Sydney says she wants to enjoy some time together just the two of them as a married couple. I swear, those two. Relationship goals. If I had that kind of mutual adoration, I'd be one happy camper.

I glance over my shoulder at a scowling Adam. Instead I have a man who wants to pretend he barely knows me at a barbecue, even though we've spent every spare minute together for more than a month. Plus we had that fake-fiancé date, and a very nice time the week before that at Wyatt's wedding. Why, it's practically been two months we've been together and months before that as friends.

Why did I have to let my heart get involved?

Honestly, how could I not? Any woman would fall for Adam after spending as much time with him as I have. He's generous and kind and undeniably sexy. I can't expect him to meet me where I'm at when we both went into this as a casual thing. Right? That's, like, the one rule.

This sucks! I can't believe I let this happen. I nearly want to go into Wyatt's house and hide. Pretending to barely know each other at a party feels wrong. And my feelings are bruised and tender too.

Jenna approaches, her arms wide to me. She's wearing a cute white sundress that ends mid-thigh with white wedge sandals. "There you are, lady!"

I smile and hug her.

She looks over my shoulder. "And you brought your grumpy guy."

I wave toward Adam, who's definitely looking put out as he walks toward us, a six-pack of beer in one hand and Tank's leash in the other. "He's not my guy, believe me."

"Still no go?" she whispers.

"We're just friends," I say, nearly choking on the words. At Jenna's concerned look, I add, "It's fine. I'm happy."

"Liar." She hooks her arm in mine and leads me over to the group. Wyatt invited the whole Robinson family, Sydney and her four brothers—Drew, Eli, Caleb, and grumpy Adam. I also spot our tamale-making mailman, Bill (he delivers tamales with the mail in the spring and fall), and his wife,

Paula, the local shopkeeper Nicholas, who looks just like Santa, and some of the regulars from the bar.

I smile and wave. "Hi, everyone!"

Wyatt turns at my voice. "Finally. What took you so long, runt?" His thick brown hair is getting longer with an unruly wave on top. He walks over and throws an arm around my shoulders, pulling me close and kissing the top of my head. "Snowball couldn't wait to meet her new bulldog boyfriend. I'll go get her. She's lounging inside with Rexie."

"I'll get her." That could make a nice escape from tense Adam.

"It's no problem."

He leaves, striding toward the house, and my cowardly attempt to hide is thwarted. It's just that I'm so agitated about Adam and want to put space between us before I give myself away. I'm supposed to pretend we're nothing to each other as he requested. The jerk.

I hug Sydney, exclaiming over her tanned skin. Normally, she doesn't tan at all, but between her honeymoon and the long weekend she just spent with Wyatt at a rented beach house in the Hamptons, she has some color. Sydney's tough and speaks her mind like my sister Paige. I think they'd get along swimmingly. They even both have auburn hair, though Paige's color is from the salon.

Sydney lowers her voice. "Are you and Adam fighting? He looks cranky, and you seem wired."

"Nothing's changed at all. Still sort of friends, sort of not. And for some reason he doesn't want Wyatt to know we're anything at all."

She glances toward the house, probably checking for Wyatt. "Come on, you know Wyatt looks out for you. I'm sure if you were honest with him, he'd be fine with the two of you."

I purse my lips. "Adam says Wyatt warned him away from me. And, actually, Wyatt advised me not to play the fake-engagement game so I wouldn't get hurt, but if I listened to him, I never would've had this special time with Adam."

My voice chokes over the lump of emotion lodged in my throat.

She narrows her eyes, which means she's getting pissed at Wyatt.

I grab her arm. "Don't say a word to Wyatt. It's a nonissue. Seriously. Adam doesn't feel that way about me." My eyes get hot. "And I'm fine."

"Oh, Kayla," she starts.

I shake my head, not wanting sympathy. I might cry, and then Adam would see, and Wyatt would raise hell on my behalf.

Audrey appears by my side. Her long black hair is up in a messy bun. Her outfit today is unusual for her. Typically she'll wear neat blouses with Peter Pan collars and tailored trousers, maybe a loose tunic and leggings for casual wear, but today she's wearing a tight red T-shirt and a blue plaid miniskirt with flip-flops. She's rocking the outfit. "Did you read *Marriage Fellows*?" she asks. That's our book club selection.

"Sorry, I haven't gotten to it yet, but I swear I will by our Tuesday meeting." I lean close to whisper, "Cute outfit. Are you on one of your first dates?"

She's been sharing all the nitty-gritty of her dates with me. It makes me appreciate Adam even more. One guy told her he liked how short she was for several sexual reasons, which he shared in explicit detail. *On their first date.* Needless to say, she was so appalled, she left immediately. Just got up in the middle of dinner and walked out.

She sighs. "No. I meant what I said before. I'm taking a break from eLoveMatch."

"But I thought you were determined to keep searching no matter what." She's been adamant that she wants a serious relationship. She says she's more than ready for marriage and kids.

"No sparks," she says with a shrug. "Frankly, I'm exhausted by the whole dating scene."

"Translation no sex," Sydney puts in, giving Audrey's arm a squeeze.

"That too," Audrey says, even as she blushes.

I'd like to assure Audrey that sex is overrated to make us both feel better, but I don't know that for a fact. What Adam does do to me is fantastic—mind-blowing orgasms the likes of which I never knew existed. I can't say that either, even though it's just us girls. I like keeping that mind-blowing part between me and Adam. Maybe sex isn't overrated if you're with the right person. Adam and I have a strong bond formed in friendship. Dammit. I'm definitely missing out on sex.

Jenna joins us with a glass of something fruity. "Sangria is delicious, Syd. What're we talking about over here?"

"Sex," Sydney says.

"Ah, who's not getting any and who is," Jenna says knowledgably. "Consider me caught up." She winks at Sydney.

Audrey and I exchange a look. Clearly, we're the only two not getting any, though I believe I'm experiencing far more than Audrey. It's too bad she's hung up on a clueless man. I glance over at Drew, who's setting up a volleyball net with Caleb. Okay, I see the appeal. Drew's in a dark green sleeveless shirt that displays his bulging biceps nicely, his brown hair on the longish side with scruff on his jaw. He's got a bit of a tough rebel vibe going on there. Though I don't quite get why bookish librarian Audrey is hung up on him. Wouldn't she be happier with a bookish guy? Drew's way into martial arts, and he was in the military before that. He's all about the body, and she's all about the mind. Hmm…

Caleb, with his crew cut of light brown hair and clean-shaven face, seems more like Audrey's type. Cheerful guy that he is, Caleb is talking away to Drew, who barely acknowledges him with more than a jerk of the chin. I bet Drew hasn't even noticed Audrey's wearing a curve-revealing outfit today.

I tune back into my friends as Jenna shares about her bakery's latest flavors for ice cream sandwiches made with cake layers. She brought lemon cake with vanilla ice cream and passion fruit cake with coconut ice cream. Summer is the big season for cake sandwiches at her shop.

I glance around, looking for Adam. He's crouched next to Tank under the shade of the green canopy. He's avoiding me. Guess he doesn't want to tangle with me in front of everyone. I sense a fight coming. I'm just so agitated, and he's so, so frustrating.

Wyatt returns with Snowball and Rexie on leashes, and they bark up a storm, racing toward Tank.

And that big tough-looking bulldog looks alarmed. He makes a growling sound to warn them off. Adam takes over, stroking a hand over his head. "Sit." Tank sits, his big eyes still glued to the strange dogs.

Wyatt guides his dogs over and hands a small biscuit to Tank and then to Snowball and Rexie. He starts talking to Adam, and the dogs sniff each other, making a funny, twisty circle as they sniff each other's butts.

Adam's gaze meets mine and holds for an intense moment.

What does that mean? Does he want me to go to him? Is he still mad? I can't tell. The man is a frigging mystery. It must be all my emotions getting in the way of translating Adam speak like I used to.

Wyatt's gaze follows Adam's, and he jerks his chin at me in acknowledgment. They can have their manly conversation without me. I'm just fine with Sydney, Jenna, and Audrey.

I do my best to focus on the conversation, but my eyes trail to Adam over and over. He's mostly hanging with Wyatt, the two of them talking with a beer in hand. Adam smiles, and I realize he must really like my brother. Adam doesn't smile all that much. Except with me.

A short while later, we all help ourselves to lunch. Adam sits across from me at a long glass patio table, his gaze heated. I instantly flush. That's all it takes between us—one hot look.

I avoid his eyes as I eat my lunch, a grilled chicken sandwich and salad. I do my best to talk to Audrey by my side, but I can feel his eyes on me.

When I finish eating, I look up.

Adam gestures with his head toward the house, his kissable lips curving up slightly. I read that signal loud and clear. Nope. We're not going to fool around now. First of all, we're at a party. Second, Wyatt's not supposed to know about us for some insane reason. Like it's horrible that I have fun with a man. Third, I'm mad at Adam for...I don't know. Everything! Not letting me get close physically, being casual now when we've been spending so much time together. I can't be the only one with feelings in this thing, can I?

"I thought you were mad at me," I whisper to Adam.

Conversation quiets around us as ears perk up.

He stands, clearing his plate and plastic flatware. "I was never mad at you," he mutters before heading toward the house.

I do the same, following him. I hear Wyatt ask, "Why would Adam be mad at her?"

Sydney's reply is quiet, but she must've said something that sounded reasonable to Wyatt's ears because he doesn't follow me.

I catch up with Adam in the kitchen, which is a bright modern space with white cabinets, a huge granite-topped island, and stainless steel appliances. Adam looks out of place in his black T-shirt and jeans. I can almost see the tool belt normally hanging low on his hips. He belongs in a workshop space or standing in sawdust. My whole life I've been drawn to intellectual types, yet only Adam sparks passion in me. And so much more.

His back is to me as he closes the under-cabinet trash bin. I join him, and he slides it open for me and closes it again.

He slants a sideways look at me. "You were mad at me, not the other way round."

I keep my voice low. "You said our friendship was abnormal."

"You said the way we fool around was abnormal."

Audrey wanders in. "Great weather we're having, huh?" Her voice sounds high and overly cheerful. She must've overheard and is trying to cover up the awkward. She tosses her plate in the bin and helps herself to a spiked seltzer from the refrigerator.

"Sure is," I say to Audrey, playing along. Audrey and I are beyond talking about the weather between us.

I gesture for Adam to follow me to the library in the next room. It's where our friendship began. Adam built most of it, from the bookshelves to the cabinetry, crown molding, wall trim, and a ladder that rolls on wheels. He even restored the hardwood floor, replacing some planks and making them blend seamlessly. He's a true artist.

I step into the room and hear the door shut behind me. A shiver of excitement races down my spine. We're alone. *No, you are not here to make out with him. It's time you had a talk. A serious talk.* He needs to know I don't want to be friends with half a benefit anymore. I want to share everything with him, physically, emotionally. I want it all.

He steps close, his eyes smoldering into mine, and my mind goes blank. He pins me against the door, his fingers spearing through my hair, holding me in place as his mouth plunders. A rush of lust makes me woozy. His mouth trails to my neck as his hand slides up my dress. I should stop him, but I'm weak with lust. Desire pools between my legs, and he pushes my panties to the side, his mouth covering mine as his fingers stroke me intimately.

I'm caught on the Adam ride, pleasure rocketing through me as I race to release. He swallows my soft cries, his knowing fingers working me. I jerk as the orgasm hits, rocking mindlessly against his hand. He guides me all the way to the last spark of pleasure until I go limp.

I lean back against the door, panting, as he adjusts my dress.

He kisses my throat, his teeth scraping against the cord of my neck before whispering in my ear, "Normal is overrated."

I laugh a little. "I can't resist you."

He meets my eyes. "Same."

"It should be mutual. I'm ready. I want it to be you." *And more. I want all of you.*

"You don't."

"Yes, I do."

"You think you do, but you don't."

Despair immediately dampens my afterglow. He's never going to let me in.

I push him away from me. "Don't tell me what I'm thinking. I know my mind!"

I open the door and rush out, nearly running into Wyatt.

"Are you okay, runt?" Wyatt asks and then looks over my shoulder to Adam, who was obviously just alone in the library with me. "What were you doing in the library together?"

13

Adam

Shit. This is exactly what Wyatt warned me not to do. He said only get involved if it's serious. Kayla is the marrying type. I couldn't help it. Kayla was avoiding me, and I knew if I could get her alone, I could remind her why she likes spending so much time with me. I couldn't stand her being mad at me.

"Nothing," Kayla says to Wyatt, which is obviously untrue. Her hair is mussed by my hands, her face and chest flushed from her recent orgasm, even her lips are red. Those pouty sexy lips.

"Oh, hey, guys," Sydney says, appearing at Wyatt's side. "We're about to make teams for volleyball, you in?"

"Just a minute," Wyatt says, sparing Sydney a brief glance. "Adam was just about to explain what he's doing in the library with my sister."

Sydney presses her lips together, fighting back a smile. *Did Kayla tell her about us?* That's risky. She could easily spill to Wyatt.

"It's not a big deal, Wyatt," Kayla says, waving toward the library. "I was just looking around, admiring his woodwork. It's been a while since I've been in here."

"Admiring his wood, huh?" Sydney quips. "I've heard that one before."

Wyatt shoots her a dark look.

"It's nothing," I say. "We're friends."

Wyatt steps closer to Kayla, inspecting her neck. He jabs a finger at her. "Then why does she have whisker burn on her neck?"

I peer at her. It's a mark from my teeth, actually, but I don't think he'll appreciate the clarification.

"So we made out a little," Kayla says. "Happy now? Let's go play volleyball."

"No, I'm not happy," Wyatt says. "I'm the one who helped you put yourself back together after you were left at the altar. I *knew* I shouldn't have let you play the fake-engagement game. This is what happens." He pins me with a hard look. "And I specifically told you to leave her alone unless you're serious. Are you serious?"

"No," I admit.

Kayla's shoulders droop as she stares at the floor. I instantly wish I could take it back. It's not casual, but it's not serious either. I don't know what it is, but I can't seem to stop being with her. I don't even care about pretending to be engaged anymore. All I care about is Kayla with her beaming smiles and sunny personality. She's so easy to be with.

"Kayla," I start.

She holds up a hand, her chin jutting out. "Yup. Casual." She walks out on stiff legs, and Sydney follows her.

Wyatt grabs me by the shirt. "What did you do? She's upset. Did you make her promises like it was serious?"

"No." I knock his hand off me. "She's fine. She agreed it's casual."

"Do I have to teach you Women 101? Her tone was all wrong, and she walked out of the room stiff-legged. She's upset, genius."

I look over to where Kayla just left and turn back to him. "Look, I'd never hurt her."

"You already did. God, I'd punch you in the face if you

weren't so damn clueless. Just stay away from her from now on."

He turns and leaves.

The hell with that. I did nothing wrong. I went out of my way to make sure Kayla had no regrets when it came to our time together. I've only ever given her pleasure. And she's returned the favor just by being her sweet bubbly self.

I take a few moments to consider my next move and arrive outside to chaos.

The green canopy is half-collapsed, the food on the patio table is scattered everywhere, and everyone's running around chasing Snowball and Rexie.

I go over to the table, where Caleb and Jenna are cleaning up the mess with paper towels. "What happened?"

"Dogs made an escape," Jenna says. "They were all tied to the same canopy pole and made a break for the food when no one was looking."

Had to be Tank. He's very food motivated and strong. I guess someone tied Snowball and Rexie to the same pole, and Tank probably pulled hard enough to set them all free.

Wyatt's screaming like a desperate man for Snowball in the woods. Drew, Audrey, and a few others are going for Rexie, who's running in a weird zigzag pattern all over the expansive lawn.

I look under the table. There's Tank, lying down with his head on his paws, looking content. A mangled plastic plate is next to him, along with scattered corn kernels. He doesn't like corn. "What did you do?"

He lifts his brows as if to say *problem?* And then closes his eyes and goes to sleep.

I don't bother with his leash. He's not going anywhere. I straighten. "How much food was out?"

"Mostly a variety of salads," Caleb says, indicating the mess. "Not too popular with the dogs. I'd say there were four hot dogs left."

"And a couple of burgers," Jenna says. "Sydney was just starting to put stuff away when she saw Wyatt go inside, noticed you and Kayla hadn't come out yet, and went in to hold off a showdown."

Caleb grins. "Was there a showdown?"

I shrug and look off in the distance as the humans yell and run while the dogs look like they're enjoying a game of chase. "He's not happy." *Neither is Kayla.*

"He'll come around," Jenna says. "He just has to get used to his baby sister having a…" She winks. "Social life."

She was about to say sex life. It occurs to me Kayla has shared our private stuff with her friends. Not cool. Kayla always says whatever's on her mind whenever. There are limits. I need to have a talk with her.

I walk away, heading over to Sydney. "Does Kayla share stuff about us?"

"Yeah, but don't worry. It's all covered in the sisterhood code. I haven't said a word to Wyatt." She shakes her head, smiling, as Wyatt dodges to the right to catch Snowball, and the dog goes left, neatly avoiding him. Wyatt stumbles and barely rights himself in time, before taking off after her again, Snowball's leash flying behind her.

I clench my jaw. "That's private. I can't believe she told you stuff."

"Your woman is an open book. Be glad. You'll always know what she's thinking."

Except I don't get what she's so mad about. I watch as Kayla crouches down, coaxing Rexie to go to her, who looks like she's thinking about it, until Drew comes up behind Rexie. She takes off again, running around the side of the house.

Sydney whistles sharply. "Rexie, come." The dog runs straight to Sydney's side, panting and looking up at her adoringly. "Good girl," Sydney murmurs, taking her leash. "Enough playtime."

She turns and yells, "Wyatt, I got Rexie. Stop running after Snowball. She thinks you're playing."

"I have to get her back!" He turns. "Snowball, come! I'm not fooling around!" She breaks from the tree line and runs toward the grassy lawn.

Wyatt runs after her, dives for her leash, and grabs it. Snowball twists and takes off, her harness popping right off. A blur of little white fur zips past us, running toward the house.

Wyatt takes off like a maniac after her. "Snowball, come!"

"This is where an electric fence could help!" Sydney yells.

Wyatt barely breaks stride. "Snowball is too sensitive for a shock!"

"Such a softie," Sydney murmurs.

Snowball gets to the patio door and paws it to be let in. Wyatt opens the door and shuts it behind them, bending at the waist to catch his breath, and giving Sydney a thumbs-up.

"Gotta love his dedication to those he loves," Sydney says dreamily before joining him with Rexie.

A few minutes later, they return with the dogs outside and get Snowball back into her harness.

Wyatt clips a square plastic tag to Snowball's collar. "I don't know why I didn't think of this before. GPS tracker is better than an electric fence any day. Syd, take the tracker I gave you off your keychain and put it on Rexie's collar. I'll order more."

"That's a great idea," Kayla calls over. "Dog trackers." And then she pulls her keychain out of her purse, removes the square tracker, and puts it on Tank's collar.

My chest aches. She's such a caring person, looking out for my dog. I don't think I've ever met someone as caring as she is.

It's going to suck when she leaves for her new job.

Once the food's cleaned up, the canopy put away, and the dogs safely inside, Sydney and Drew start to divide us up into volleyball teams. They're both super competitive when it comes to games, and they're picking out tall people for the advantage.

Wyatt's already on Sydney's team, and the tall math teacher, Steve, is on Drew's team.

Sydney chooses me, and Drew immediately chooses Caleb. I watch as everyone is divvied up until it's just down to Audrey and Kayla, the short ones. I tried to get Sydney to choose Kayla, but she shooed me away. It must be insulting for those two. Even the old guy, Nicholas, was chosen before them.

Audrey's eyes are locked on Drew, willing him to choose her. It's his turn to pick.

"Audrey," he says.

She does a little hop and heads over to his team. He gestures for her to go up front close to the net.

Kayla wanders over to our side.

"No offense," Sydney says. "You're just short."

"I could be good at volleyball," Kayla returns. "You don't know."

Sydney checks in with Wyatt, who shakes his head. Sydney turns her back to Kayla and gestures me forward with a subtle wiggle of her fingers. She wants me to cover for Kayla. I'm happy to. I go up front next to her.

Good thing too. She keeps missing the ball or not hitting it hard enough to get over the net. I'm there to save it. We're a team.

We win, and I offer her a high five. She doesn't return it. "Adam, I could've done those shots myself."

"You just needed an assist."

"I didn't."

Wyatt scowls at me and puts his arm around her shoulders, guiding her away. Seriously? He doesn't have to intervene. She's fine.

Only things get worse. Kayla's snippy with me for the rest of the party, and I know we're going to have an uncomfortable drive back. She probably won't even want to stop by my place, even though we've gotten used to watching a movie on Sunday nights with popcorn and Tank curled up by our feet. It's strange how quickly I've gotten used to having her in my life.

I can tell it's not going to go well the moment she gets in my car. She glances back at Tank. "Tank had a good time."

"You didn't?"

"It would've been better without Wyatt's interference, dontcha think?"

I make a quick K-turn and pull out of the driveway, surprised at her assessment. I thought she was mad at me when she's mad at her brother. "I told him not to worry about it. We both agreed it's casual."

"Right. It means nothing. Just fooling around. Half benefits."

"Yeah," I say slowly, though it feels awful to hear her say it means nothing. It means something, right? "We just like being together, and sometimes we cross the line, but it's nothing that couldn't be uncrossed at any moment."

"Well, that's the important thing, isn't it?" she asks brightly. "No permanent damage done."

"What's wrong?"

"Nothing. Everything's great."

"It doesn't sound great."

"No, it is. I wanted casual. You obviously want the same thing, so there's no problem here."

I glance at her, unsure what to say. Agreeing seems the only way to go. "Right."

She huffs. "I can't take this anymore."

"Take what?"

"It's my fault," she mutters. "I brought this on myself. I said one thing, thinking it was fine, and then it got weird, and I'm still a frigging virgin, and nothing is turning out anywhere near fine."

"Do you not want to fool around anymore, is that the problem? 'Cause that's okay by me. We can go back to being friends. That's always an option."

She gets quiet.

It's unnerving, but I have no idea what to say. I'm not even sure what the problem is.

A few minutes later, I pull up to my street.

"No, I want to go home," she says.

I pull around the cul-de-sac and head toward her place. "I

don't get the problem. We agreed it's casual. Is it not casual anymore?"

"It's not anything." She looks out the window. "I can't see you anymore, okay?"

"Even as friends?"

"We were never friends," she mutters.

"The hell we weren't. You insisted on being my friend. We talked for months before we crossed the line. You think I let just anyone in?"

Her head whips toward me. "See? You think this screwed-up situation is all my fault too."

"It's not screwed up. It's fine."

"Nothing is fine, and the fact that you think that is *exactly* the problem."

I'm so confused. I park at The Horseman Inn and look at her. I don't know how to fix this because I don't get what changed. Everything seemed fine, and then suddenly it's not.

She leans over and kisses my cheek. "Bye, Adam."

My stomach drops at the words, everything in me protesting. It sounds like a breakup. How can that be when we were never a couple? "Kayla."

She shakes her head, opens the door, and races to the back of the restaurant to her apartment entrance. I'm tempted to follow her, but I don't know what I'd say to convince her we don't have to end. Not completely.

Tank makes a doggy whine from the back seat like he's upset that we just lost our best friend. *Me too, buddy.*

~

Adam

I haven't seen Kayla in two days, and I miss her with an ache that just won't stop. I miss her beaming smile, her sparkling eyes, her cheerful talk. Somehow the two of us fell into a relationship.

Okay, I get that she's frustrated with me. I've been holding her off from sex, trying to let her wait for the guy she'll one day meet and marry.

I'm not looking for marriage. She even said we wouldn't be compatible that way.

I just need to talk to her again.

I show up at The Horseman Inn on Tuesday night. I'm not sure if she's working tonight. If she's not, I'll try her apartment.

I greet the host with a brief nod, scanning the front dining room for her, and then continue on to the back room. No Kayla. And then I hear her laugh and spot her standing next to the table in the back, where my brother Drew likes to sit when he watches the game.

I shift to see his expression. He's actually smiling at her. Anger spikes through me. I'm mad because Drew knows Kayla's *my* friend, and I'm mad at Kayla because that's my brother. Is she so frustrated with me that she's propositioning him? She did say she thought he was great the way he looked out for Sydney and checked on the restaurant regularly. I hate that I'm jealous.

She pulls out her phone and taps on it, listening to him intently. She's getting his number.

I take a step forward, ready to intervene, and then I remember I have no hold on her. She told me goodbye. She said she couldn't do this *whatever it is* with me anymore.

I can't stand to watch. I turn and stride quickly out of the restaurant. I don't know what I thought would happen. I had no speech planned. I just wanted to see her.

Now I have the gut-churning, chest-aching horrible feelings to show for it.

Perfect.

I make it through the rest of the week in a fog, my mind replaying every conversation with Kayla at my place, at the lake, at Clover Park, and around Summerdale. I'm trying to figure out where it went wrong. She said she wanted me to take her virginity. I said let's wait a month.

Now it's more than a month and she's mad.

Okay, so she's frustrated, but now she doesn't want to see me anymore, so how does she expect me to help her out if we don't see each other? How does that make sense?

She said she didn't want me to think of her as the kind of woman you marry. She even gave me every reason we weren't compatible. What did she say? Something like: *I'm very talkative, and you prefer quiet. I like character-driven dramas; you like boring baseball. I love to dance and have fun at parties; you like to work your wood. We have nothing in common besides our siblings.*

Those things are still true, I guess. But some of those kind of work together. I like listening to her talk. Sure, we don't like to watch the same shows, but I like having her pressed up against my side when we watch TV no matter what's on. And I don't mind doing things that are fun for her because I want her to be happy. And she admires my carpentry work. I'm sure I could admire her biostatistician work with its pattern of numbers. Or at least I'd appreciate it because it's what she's good at.

I think back to Amelia. I've only seen her a few times at the lake on my walks with Kayla and Tank and felt nothing. What did we used to have in common? Why did I think we'd work as a married couple? The sex was explosive, usually after a fight. Amelia used to harp on me about not talking much, always asking me what I was thinking, like my silence indicated something against her. She always wanted reassurance that I loved her. Even though I thought inviting her to live with me showed that. Now that I think back on it, we didn't have much in common at all. She likes travel, new experiences, meeting new people all the time. I like a quiet life in a town that has everything I ever wanted—community, family, nature.

I go through the motions of microwaving dinner and eating, barely tasting the chicken parmigiana and noodles. Does it really matter exactly how much we have in common? Isn't it more important that we're compatible? Kayla and I complement each other. She accepts the way I am, and I love the way she is.

I gulp, my fork stilling. I love her.

I leap from my seat, startling Tank into a low growl.

How did I not see it before? I love being with her, love talking to her, love giving her pleasure. So much so, I ask for nothing in return. It's an insult to her. That's the problem. She wants to give back, and I push her away every time. It's not just physical. It's way beyond that. It's about true intimacy between two people who are way beyond friends.

I have to tell her. It's Friday night. She always works Friday and Saturday nights. I'll go to The Horseman Inn, wait for her break, and go upstairs with her to lay it all on the line. We don't have to say goodbye.

I make it to the restaurant in record time, my breath shallow as urgency drives me on. I didn't have time to come up with a speech, but I'm just going to make my case for why we're compatible and what that means.

I burst inside, looking for her. I don't see her in the front room. I move to the back of the restaurant, looking quickly back and forth. Still no Kayla. I'm about to try her apartment when Sydney finishes checking on a customer and walks over to me. "Hey, Adam, you okay? You look like you were just chased in here, sort of panicky."

"Where is she?"

She doesn't pretend not to know who I mean. "Don't you guys talk? She's in Indiana. The company liked her so much for the phone interview, they flew her out for a second interview."

"Indiana," I echo. It's far. I'd have to fly to get to her quickly, and the rush ticket will be expensive. I'll pay it. I don't care. But what if I fly out there while she's flying back here? "When's she coming back?"

"So you're not hanging out anymore?"

"Just tell me!"

"Okay, chill. Geez, I've never seen you like this. Take a breath, okay? She's staying for a week. She had an all-day interview today that went really well, and she's staying to explore the area and visit her college roommate."

Adrenaline kicks in. She's going to get a job offer far from here. I knew this was a possibility, it's the only reason I got as involved as I did, and now that it's here, I can't bear it. "Okay, where exactly in Indiana? I need her friend's address."

"I really feel like this is something you need to talk to Kayla about."

I grab her arm, my voice low. "I'm losing her. I can't lose her, Syd."

Her eyes widen. "Oh, wow, you fell for her, didn't you? I'm so happy—"

"Address," I say through my teeth.

She pulls her phone out and pulls up a hotel name. "She's got a nice suite, all paid for by the bigwig pharmaceutical company."

I snap a picture of the info and take off.

"I'm rooting for you, bro!" she yells after me. There's a murmur of curious voices behind me.

I don't have time to waste. I can't lose her forever.

14

Kayla

I finish my long luxurious shower in the marble bathroom of my deluxe hotel room and sigh. This is the life. Such a far cry from the tiny shower stall with minimal water pressure at my apartment. Noon Pharmaceuticals paid for me to stay in this gorgeous room with a view of downtown Indianapolis. The bathroom has a soaking tub and enclosed shower, complimentary luxury bath and beauty products, thick white towels, heated towel racks. Truly a sumptuous space. It went really well at my interview yesterday. I spent the entire day meeting with a lot of different people, all the way up to the VP of research and development. I think they're going to make me an offer. They said they'd get back to me on Monday.

I pad into the main room, which is also spacious and lovely. There's a king-size bed with a fluffy white down comforter, along with a sitting area with a sofa and a desk. Brunch should be here in half an hour from room service. Nothing better than a Belgian waffle to start your day. I'm meeting up with my friend Livvie tonight for dinner and drinks. She's a mom with a toddler at home now, and she's dying to have a night out. She married right out of college to the guy she met the first day on campus. She says it was like a lightning strike with Justin. They instantly knew.

I wish things were that clear for me. I seem to stumble along in relationships, never sure where I stand, afraid to ask and come off like I'm pressuring a guy. Maybe it just hasn't happened for me yet—that lightning strike. Though there was something special with Adam from the very first time I clapped eyes on him last January. He stopped by Wyatt's house to help remove a fallen tree, and I couldn't stop staring at him. I wasn't ready for any kind of involvement with a guy at the time, but I couldn't resist visiting him the following week when he started his carpentry work for Wyatt. We were friends because that's all I could handle, and it seemed like that was all he needed too. And then it changed. I changed it, and now it's ruined. We're not even friends anymore.

My eyes well, and I shake my head at myself. I've cried enough about him. I'm the one with the problem. I changed the rules, he didn't want anything serious, and I can't expect him to magically be where I'm at.

I sniffle and get dressed in a summery pink off-the-shoulder top with white shorts and sandals. After my Belgian waffle with whipped cream, I plan on exploring the downtown.

I return to the bathroom, wipe off the mirror so I can see myself through the condensation, and carefully apply makeup. Even if I feel wretched on the inside, I want to look put together on the outside. I haven't seen Livvie in a couple of years, and I want her to think I have it together. I do, mostly. I'm on my way to finally starting a career after years of school. That's a big deal. I don't want her to take one look at me and think, what happened?

I wander out to the room, open the curtains, and take in all the tall buildings. So different from the lakeside community I've grown to love. There must be a lake around here somewhere. I'd miss not having a lake.

The hotel phone on the nightstand rings, startling me. I wonder if there's a problem with my room service order. Damn, I was really looking forward to a Belgian waffle.

I pick up the phone. "Hello?"

"Hello, Ms. Winters. You have a visitor. Adam Robinson. Would you like me to send him up?"

My hand flies to my mouth. Adam? Here? How did he even know where I was?

"Ma'am?"

"Yes. Send him up, please."

I thank him and hang up, my heart racing. I look around in a panic and quickly make the bed, hang up my bath towel, and straighten up my toiletries. What am I doing? Like Adam cares if my hotel room is neat. I can't believe he's here! Sydney must've told him where I was.

I wring my hands together. What does this mean?

I pace the room and then open the door, searching for him, too wired to wait. The elevator dings, and he steps out, his jaw set. He's got a duffel bag over one shoulder.

"Adam."

He marches toward me, his expression serious. "We need to talk."

"I can't believe you're here."

"Got the first flight out this morning. Sydney told me where you were."

I step back to let him in. "Have a seat." I gesture toward the sofa, which is small, more like a love seat.

He drops his duffel bag by the door and strides over to the sofa, flopping down.

I join him on the sofa. "Are you okay?"

He leans forward, resting his elbows on his knees. "No, I'm not. I haven't been okay since you told me goodbye six days ago." He levels a hard look at me. "Six days, Kayla."

My lips part in surprise. He must've missed me.

He straightens and meets my eyes intently. "I just want you to hear me out, let me make my case, and then you decide what you want to do."

A small ray of hope warms me. "Okay."

"First, we're very compatible. I know you said we weren't because you talk and I listen, but that complements each other. And, not only that, it doesn't matter if we watch the same TV shows as long as we're sitting together. That's all I need. To hold your hand or feel you pressed against my side. And I'll go to as many parties as you want. I'll even dance with you. All I want is your happiness."

My throat tightens, and I take a deep breath to loosen it. "It sounds like—"

"I'm not done. We're compatible physically too. I've never wanted another woman the way I want you, and I held you off, convinced you'd regret it because I was not the one who'd be sticking by you, but the thing is, Kayla, I want to stick. I've never wanted anything more. So if it's still okay with you, I'd like to be your first."

Pure happiness bubbles up inside me. "Oh, Adam, I—"

"And your last. What I'm saying is, we should get married."

I stare at him, shocked. "We should get married? Why?"

"Because we're compatible in every way, and I want you to have that security. Your first, your last."

Because of sex. Not one mention of love. He's still trying to protect me in his misguided way. He's saying he knows what's best for me. We *should* get married.

I shake my head.

"What's no? You don't want to marry me?"

I stand. "It's just not right. I'm sorry. I think you should go."

He doesn't move, his brows knit together.

Do I have to spell it out? You don't love me. That's the only reason I'd consider getting married. I'm saved from pointing out the horrible truth by a knock on the door.

"Who's that?" he asks.

"I assume room service," I say.

He goes to answer the door for me, and I follow. He opens the door to a smiling middle-aged guy in the hotel's maroon uniform. "Hello, room service."

Adam lets him in, and the server sets up brunch for me on the desk.

I sign it to the room. "Thank you. Have a good day."

"You too, ma'am."

The door shuts behind him.

Adam steps close. "Have you been with someone else? Is that why you don't want me anymore? Is it too late to be your first?"

I back away, stunned. "It's been six days!"

"I don't know. I saw you talking to Drew at the restaurant."

"So? I talk to him all the time. Other people too. If you haven't noticed, I'm a people person."

"He smiled at you."

I throw my hands up. "People smile! It doesn't mean they had sex!"

"What were you two talking about?"

I plant my hands on my hips and give him my best glare. "If you must know, he was inviting me to a free trial karate class for adult beginners, which I went to on Wednesday night. I enjoyed punching a punching bag and learning defensive maneuvers that will take down a much larger body." I eye his towering size. "I could probably take you to the ground with what I know now."

His lips twitch. "You could try."

"Glad you're amused, Adam. I'm not. You flew all this way to tell me we should get married because we're compatible. Well, I don't agree. I'm compatible with a lot of people I won't be marrying. I'm compatible with the VP of Noon Pharmaceuticals research, won't be marrying him. I'm compatible with the research associate I followed yesterday, won't be marrying him. I'm compatible with Audrey, won't be marrying her."

"I'm sensing the word compatible is the problem."

I turn and walk over to my brunch. "I'm going to eat. I'm feeling very hangry."

"Okay. I'll wait."

"No, you should go."

"I'm not going anywhere."

I bite back what I want to say, which is *clueless man!* How can we be in two such different places?

I take a few bites of waffle and then turn to where he's

standing looking out the window. "You want a bite?"

"I'm good."

I go back to eating, but I don't enjoy it at all. I just need my strength to deal with Adam. I'm finally going to admit I have deep feelings and, if he doesn't return them, then we need to say goodbye for good.

"They put you up in a nice hotel," he says. "They must really want you on board."

"I'll hear on Monday. It's a good job with potential for growth long term. They have all sorts of interesting ways I could branch out too."

"Have you had any other job offers?"

"This would be the first. Though I do have second interviews scheduled at others."

"Any close to home?"

"Close enough to visit. New Jersey, Boston, Manhattan, none easily commutable."

He nods and crosses his arms.

I'm tired of hoping he'll say something deep. He says he missed me but that's all. Maybe he just misses our friends-with-half-a-benefit relationship. I finish breakfast and cover the plate with the silver domed lid. Then I drink my water and turn my swivel chair to face him.

The words lodge in my throat. I take a deep breath and blurt, "I can't do friends with half a benefit with you anymore."

He steps closer. "I'm saying we can be friends with full benefits, and I think we should get married too."

I take a deep breath. "I don't think we should get married just because of that. You're not responsible for what I thought I wanted before—sex only with my husband. I've changed my mind. That's not what I want anymore."

He sits on the edge of the desk next to me, his voice fierce. "I don't want you to have sex with anyone else."

I close my eyes, pained over the complete disconnect with the man I'm in love with. "I'm afraid sex has become this huge deal between us, having it, not having it." I open my eyes. "Sex is not the problem."

"Tell me what is."

My lower lip wobbles, tears springing to my eyes. "The problem is, I have deep feelings for you, and you have nothing but obligation toward me and what you think I need when all I want is to be close to you. And I don't mean physically close, okay?"

He pulls me out of my chair and wraps his arms around me. "You are close to me."

I press my cheek against his chest, listening to the solid thump of his heart. "It doesn't feel like it. It feels like you keep me at a distance in every way." I lift my head. "It's my fault. I changed the rules. I can't help it. Any woman who spent any amount of time with you would fall for you."

He tips my chin up. "Sweet woman. What I was trying to say in my bumbling way before was this, I'm all in now. I love you."

My lower lip trembles. "Really?"

He rubs his thumb across my lower lip. "Yeah, really. You think I just blurt out the L word to anyone?"

I kiss him, tears springing to my eyes. I wipe them away. "Statistically speaking, you're unlikely to lose me. I love you so much."

"Kayla." He holds me tight like he never wants to let me go.

"This is the first time you've ever hugged me first. I'm always the one hugging you."

"I was an idiot before, trying to keep you at a distance." He frames my face with both hands. "And then you were at a distance, and I couldn't bear the thought of losing you."

I pepper his gorgeous face with kisses. "You won't. And I will marry you. Your earlier proposal counts."

"No, it doesn't. I did that all wrong with the compatibility stuff. How about you move in with me, and we'll take it from there?"

"With full benefits?"

He gives me a slow sexy smile. "We can get started on full benefits right now."

"Then you need to strip."

15

I close the curtains so all of Indianapolis doesn't get the show I'm about to get. "Nice and slow," I tell him, taking a seat on the sofa. "Make it like a stripper routine."

He chuckles and pulls off his T-shirt, spinning it over his head. "This is much tawdrier than I imagined."

"Woo! Take it all off!"

He tosses the shirt to me.

I catch it and breathe it in. "I've missed this. You always smell so good. Clean and woodsy." I grin. "Remember what you told me about seduction and stripping?"

One corner of his mouth lifts. "If you strip, he's on board. If he strips first, run."

I nod. "You stripped first, and there's no way I'm running. I'm on board."

"Me too." He kicks off his shoes and socks and rests his fingers on the button of his jeans, his eyes intent on mine. "Have you ever seen a man naked?"

"Not in real life," I admit.

"C'mere."

I go to him, and he pulls me close, his lips meeting mine. He takes my hand, running it over the length of him, letting me feel him through his jeans. It's an impressive bulge. A lick of panic runs through me. How's that going to fit?

I break the kiss and stare at it. "Show me."

He groans. "I probably shouldn't have kissed you. This would've been easier." He undoes the button and carefully unzips, pulling his jeans away from his massive erection.

I don't hesitate, grabbing the waistband of his black boxer briefs and pushing them down along with the jeans. His cock rears up, thick and engorged. I stroke it tentatively with one finger.

He groans and steps back, stripping his jeans and briefs completely off.

I bite my lower lip. "What do you like?"

"Just touch me. I'll like anything you do because it's you."

Reassured, I step close, roaming my palms over his heated chest, over defined abs, and then lower, following the trail back to his cock. I run my fingers over it, under it, around it, learning the feel of him the way he learned me. I look up at him to see how he likes it.

His expression is strained, his breath coming harder. His eyes are half-lidded as he takes my hand and guides it to circle him and stroke up and down. I watch him closely. He definitely likes that.

"I want to taste you the way you taste me," I whisper, dropping to my knees in front of him.

He grips my hair. "Kayla."

I run my tongue along the length of him and then circle the tip. Salty. And then I take him fully into my mouth, moving the way he liked with my hand. His fingers tighten in my hair, and I look up at him. His head's tipped back, his jaw tight.

I release him. "Am I hurting you?"

He grabs me, pulling me to my feet. "It feels too good."

I smile widely, thrilled I'm already good at this. "No such thing as too good."

"I want you."

"You have—" His mouth silences me with a fierce kiss, hard and demanding, so different from his usual tender kisses. Exciting. My fingers tighten on his shoulders, my world tilting as his tongue thrusts in my mouth, his hands all over me, stroking down my back, my bottom, up my sides, cupping my breasts.

I break the kiss to pull off my shirt, but he's faster. He strips me in between urgent kisses, pausing only long enough to stroke my exposed skin before going for the next piece of clothing. I'm on fire. Finally, we're both naked, and I throw my arms around his neck, kissing him passionately.

He backs me up, and the back of my knees bump into the mattress. We come up for air, both of us breathing heavily. He strips the blanket off.

His voice is hoarse. "Lie down and spread your legs for me."

I crawl over to the center of the bed, hearing his muffled groan. I peek at him over my shoulder. His eyes are heated, taking me in from that angle. "I'm all yours, Adam. Just like I always wanted to be."

"What you do to me," he mutters before snagging his jeans from the floor. He retrieves a condom from his wallet.

I'd forgotten about that. I don't have any with me. I lie in the center of the bed and spread my legs for him.

He covers me a moment later, kissing me tenderly. He lifts his head, pushing my hair back from my face. "I'll go slow for you."

"This has been weeks and weeks of slow. I don't need that anymore. Kiss me like you did before, like you want me desperately."

"I do want you desperately."

I grab his ass and pull. It's no use; he's strong and stable. He shifts close, but not where I want him, but then he distracts me, his mouth hungry and demanding again. Kiss after kiss, hot and wet and deep. There's nothing but his heat, his taste, the weight of him covering me. And then his mouth trails along my jaw, the cord of my neck, his teeth scraping against me. A hot shiver races through me.

He lowers himself down, taking his time once again, his hand cupping my breast and lifting it to his mouth. I gasp as he suckles, drawing in sharp tugs that make me throb. I spear my fingers through his hair, holding him to me, needing more, aching to be filled at the same time.

He shifts to the other breast, sucking tightly as his hand slides down to delve between my legs. My breath shudders out, the throbbing need almost unbearable. I've waited so long for this.

He kisses his way down my body, dropping kisses on my stomach, the inside of my thigh, all the way down to my toes.

"Adam." I reach for him, needing him back on top of me, wanting him to join with me.

He crawls back up me. "Not yet." He brushes his lips over mine. "Roll over for me."

"Why?"

"For more exploring." He flips me over before I can ask any more questions. He pushes my hair to the side and kisses the back of my neck, his teeth closing over my nape. Heat flashes through me like lightning, racing down my spine. His palms run over my back, followed by his mouth kissing gently down my spine. I melt into the mattress. He continues down over the curve of my bottom and down one leg, stroking, kissing, tasting. Then the other leg. I wait breathlessly. What's next?

He rolls me over and nips my lower lip, jolting me. This is a side of Adam he hasn't shown me before, rougher, more aggressive. This is Adam letting himself feel the sharp edge of need and taking what he wants. I spread my legs, pulling him by the shoulders, but he resists, lowering himself to kiss me right on the throbbing pleasure center only he's touched.

And then he surprises me, putting my legs over his shoulders and spreading me wide to his gaze. I'm pinned, open to him. My breath comes harder, my heart pounding as his heated eyes meet mine. And then he lowers his head, his mouth coaxing at first as his fingers play with me. I relax under him, my fingers tangling in his hair. The pleasure spirals higher and higher, his mouth hungry, pushing me closer to release. My breath hitches, and he gentles, my release eluding me. I moan, needing it.

And then he brings me back, climbing again, my insides

tight and hot, the intensity building. I cry out, shuddering against him, white-hot pleasure spearing through me in a starburst of pleasure all the way up to my scalp and down to my toes.

I pull on his shoulders, needing him close. He crawls up my body and lets me hug him.

"I love you, Kayla," he murmurs in my ear.

I grab his head and kiss him fiercely. "I love you too."

He positions himself at my entrance. "You're so wet, so ready for me."

I nod as he slowly pushes in, stretching me. He thrusts deep suddenly, and I gasp at the sharp pain followed by deep pressure.

He stills, one hand cradling my jaw as he kisses me. Long, lingering kisses that deepen, opening me further as he consumes me. And then he lifts his head, his gaze locked on mine as he moves slowly in and out. Suddenly I feel the love between us, something raw and real. This is making love.

"I'm so glad I waited for you," I whisper.

"It's better this way." He kisses along my jaw to my ear, taking my earlobe between his teeth and giving it a tug. "With love."

"Yes," I say softly. "Now take me like you're desperate for me."

He sucks on the cord of my neck, his thrusts slow but deep. I arch my hips, meeting each thrust. He moans against my neck before taking me harder, faster, until we're both chasing that peak. His breath is harsh by my ear as he rocks into me in just the right place.

"Adam!" I buck helplessly under him as the orgasm crashes over me. He pumps fiercely, rocking into me before letting go with a guttural groan.

He collapses on top of me, his breath coming in short pants.

My lips curve into a satisfied smile. "I finally know what all the fuss is about. That was incredibly good!"

He lifts his head. "It's not always like that."

"It's not?"

"No." He strokes a lock of hair behind my ear. "It's us, our chemistry, our love."

"Oh, Adam!" I squeeze him tight. He presses his lips to my neck, and I feel his smile against my skin.

Then he rolls off me and fixes me with a hard look. "Just us, Kayla. Got that? Just us feels like that."

He wants me all to himself. I climb on top of him and stretch out, loving this new feeling of skin on skin. I kiss him. "Only you."

His arms wrap around me in a warm hug. I wish I could stay like this forever. I don't want to think about the real world, my possible job offers, all of which take me far from him. Here, in this hotel room, is just for us.

≈

Adam

I return home late on Sunday night, tired and on edge. All I can think about is Kayla getting that job out in Indianapolis. I don't want to stand in her way. At the same time, I'd have to give up a lot to go. I have a reputation here that keeps my business thriving, mostly by word of mouth, and it's been helped even more by Wyatt's connections with the wealthy elite in the area. To be with Kayla, I'd have to sell my house, leave the community I love, my family, and start all over again from scratch.

On the other hand, I love her deeply and can't imagine my life without her.

I pull up to my house and go inside, dropping my bag by the door. Drew stopped by over the weekend to take care of Tank for me. He has the key. It's quiet. Strange. Usually Tank would greet me with at least a tired bark when I get home.

I turn on the light. Tank's not in his bed. There's a note on the coffee table. I hope he's okay. Maybe Drew had to take him to the vet. Sometimes Tank gets himself into trouble, eating the wrong thing.

I grab the note, my stomach dropping as I recognize the loopy handwriting.

. . .

Adam,

I took Tank back. I never meant for you to keep him permanently. Why should you have everything you want, and I have nothing?

Amelia

I crumple the note in my hand. Dammit. It's one a.m. I'm exhausted, torn up over Kayla, and now Amelia took my beloved Tank.

Okay, think. I pull my phone out and call Amelia. Nope, that's not her voicemail. She must've gotten a new number when she got back to the US. I call Drew, who's a night owl.

"Hey, just get in?" he asks.

"Yeah, and Tank's gone. Amelia took him. When did you last see him?"

"Shit. I took him out at ten and locked up afterward. She broke into your house?"

I look around. "She must've, or maybe one of the windows was unlocked. I don't know."

"Call Eli. He can bring her in for breaking and entering. She can't just steal your dog."

"Tank was hers to start. She has his papers."

Fuck. I was so wrapped up in Kayla, I completely forgot about paying Amelia for Tank and getting her to put something in writing that he's mine.

I tell him bye, call Eli, and then drive around the lake, looking for her red Corvette. All I know is her family rented a house by the lake. After circling the lake three times, I still don't see it. It's dark and there's no streetlights in this part of town. I'll have to try again in the morning. But what if she's already driving to parts unknown?

I rest my forehead on my steering wheel, my gut churning. I swear if she hurt Tank in any way, I'm pressing charges for animal cruelty. Though I suspect she just wants money. This is her way of getting my attention.

Then I remember Kayla put a GPS tracker on Tank after the three dogs ran away at Wyatt's barbecue. I call her, but it goes to voicemail. She doesn't respond to my text either. She's probably asleep. Indianapolis is the same time as here.

Wyatt. He's the tech whiz. If anyone could figure out where Tank is through a GPS tracker, it's him. I put the car in gear and make the short drive to Wyatt's place.

When I get to the front door, I'm relieved to see lights on inside. Hopefully that means they're up. I ring the doorbell, and the dogs set off the alarm, barking their way to the front of the house.

Wyatt opens the door a moment later, wearing a T-shirt and shorts. Snowball is tucked under his arm, Rexie standing by his side, both dogs barking at me. "Stand down. It's Adam," he commands the dogs, who instantly quiet. "Is Kayla okay?"

"She's great. I'm in love with her. Tank's missing, and I need your help."

He just stands there, staring at me.

"Didn't you hear what I said? I need your help."

He backs up to let me in. "Okay, I was just surprised. So you and Kayla are serious now?"

"Yeah."

He grins. "This is great news. Sydney told me the deal with your ex-fiancée, and I was sure you'd break Kayla's heart in self-defense." He lets out a breath. "What a relief. Okay, now I have some experience with missing dogs. I'm sure we can find him. How long's he been gone?"

Sydney appears behind him. "Hey, Adam. How'd it go in Indianapolis?"

Wyatt puts Snowball down and puts an arm around Sydney. "He's in love with her."

Sydney grins. "I knew it. When you ran out of The Horseman like a man on a mission—"

"Amelia took Tank," I say. "I have no idea where she went, and the more time passes, the farther away she can get."

"Did you search your property?" Wyatt asks. "Snowball always sticks close to the house when she makes an escape."

"My ex took him," I say slowly and clearly. "She plans to keep him." I shove a hand through my hair. "Technically she has the papers from the breeder, so I don't know how much claim I have. I offered to pay for him, but she wanted five thousand dollars, and I don't have it."

"Are you fucking kidding me?" Sydney exclaims. "You don't give that woman one cent! She gave Tank to you when she left. I remember that clearly. And we all thought she was gone for good."

"I know. I'm not sure it matters, but if she can take him from me, I can take him back. I just need to know where he is." I turn to Wyatt. "Kayla put a GPS tracker on his collar that day when the dogs got loose here. She's sleeping, so I can't get help from her, but I was hoping you could figure out how to find him."

Wyatt grins. "I bought Kayla that tracker. And I got the premium service for unlimited friends and family sharing."

Sydney gasps. "You track your sister!"

Wyatt smirks. "No, I simply share a GPS tracking service with my sisters. I can help them find their stuff, and they can help me find mine."

Sydney shakes her head. "You're totally tracking your sisters."

Wyatt cocks his head. "Paige's tracker always says she's at home. I bet she's the only one who opened the app and realized the setup." He frowns. "Now how's she going to find her keys if she loses them?"

"Wyatt, *Tank*," I say.

"Right. Let me get my phone." He heads back toward the kitchen.

Sydney and I follow him. "I never liked Amelia," she says.

"Really? You never said anything. I nearly married her."

"That's why I never said anything. You loved her and wanted to marry her. Besides, there wasn't anything I could put my finger on. She just seemed kind of fake."

I shake my head. "You should've said something. Might've saved me a lot of pain."

Sydney squeezes my arm. "I'm sorry, you're right, even though I doubt you would've taken my opinion as a reason to dump her. If it helps, I adore Kayla and think you're a great match."

If only it were that easy. "Thanks. I think so too."

"What's wrong?"

I don't want to bring up my doubts about the future, knowing Kayla might choose to live far from me. I need to focus on finding Tank.

"Just worried about Tank," I say.

Wyatt holds up his phone. "I got him. He's still in town, and I've got the address."

"Let's go," Sydney says.

"I'll call Eli," I say.

"Now we've got a posse," Wyatt says, rubbing his hands together.

And that's how the three of us end up in Wyatt's silver BMW SUV, speeding toward the rented lake house where Amelia is holding Tank hostage.

A cop car flashes its lights at us as we pull up to the house. "Ah, hell, was I speeding?" Wyatt asks, looking in the rearview.

"Definitely," Sydney says.

A moment later, my younger brother Eli appears at the driver's side window, shining a flashlight at Wyatt. Eli's in uniform and in full cop mode. No messing around. The irony is, he used to be the worst troublemaker. "Do you know why I pulled you over?"

Wyatt groans. "Come on, I'm your brother-in-law."

Eli flashes the light over the rest of us. "You were speeding, but I understand more important matters are at stake. Adam, you pressing charges against Amelia? Stolen dog, breaking and entering."

"What if we just steal Tank back?" I ask.

"You can't," Sydney says. "She'll just go for him again.

What does she really want? Is she trying to hurt you? Does she honestly love this dog?"

"She wants money," I say. "I'm sure if I paid for him, I'd never hear from her again."

"I've got money," Wyatt says. "You want me to take care of it, done deal."

"I think you should press charges and file a restraining order," Eli says.

"I think you should take something she really loves," Sydney says. "Like that Corvette. I saw her driving by the restaurant with it many times."

I consider all these angles, and then I think about everything Amelia put me through, how I almost lost Kayla over that past hurt, too defensive to risk opening my heart until it was almost too late. And now the future with Kayla is uncertain, and I only wish I hadn't held back so long. We wasted precious time.

"Let's do it all," I say. "Take Tank, press charges, file a restraining order, and let the air out of her tires." I check in with Eli. "That's not illegal, right?"

"Not by me," he says.

We head over to a small lakeside cottage with a detached garage. The Corvette is inside the garage. Sydney works open a window on the side of the garage, and Wyatt gives her a boost inside. She'll take care of the tires.

Eli and I go to the front door and ring the bell. We'll probably wake up Amelia's parents and her older sisters, if they're here, but that's her problem. Tank's familiar *oof, oof, oof* bark reaches me, and I relax. My boy. He's fine. Probably just confused and too tired to do anything but his usual nighttime snooze.

Amelia's dad, Peter, answers the door, wearing a ratty blue bathrobe. He's in his sixties with thinning gray hair. The poor guy always seems bewildered by his three daughters. "Yes?"

"Hello, Peter," I say.

He squints and gets closer. "Adam?"

"That's right."

He shakes my hand. "Good to see you again. I always thought you were a steadying influence on Amelia."

Eli pipes up, "We're here about Amelia. She's committed a few crimes she needs to answer for. Breaking and entering at Adam's place and stealing Tank here."

Tank is now curled up on a folded blanket on the floor in front of the faded green sofa.

I call him, and he merely lifts his brows and sighs. Too sleepy to realize the custody situation here. I'll probably have to carry him out.

Peter's brows shoot up. "She said you gave Tank back. As far as I'm concerned, you can keep him. That thing does nothing but whine and drool all over everything. Disgusting."

"Great," I say.

Peter grabs Tank's leash from a hook by the door, clips it on him, and tugs him over to me. Tank looks up at me with an expression of adoration before leaning heavily against my leg. He's tuckered out from all the excitement.

Amelia appears in the living room. "Dad, no! That's *my* dog."

He throws his hands in the air and stalks to the back of the house.

"I'd like to ask you a few questions," Eli says to Amelia.

"Actually, I'd like to say something first," I say. "Amelia, I know you're desperate, alone, broke, unemployed, homeless, and in a truly sad state. Maybe that's a natural consequence of choosing to run off and leave everything behind. Some might say that's punishment enough. Not me. Because not only did you end things in a heartless cheating way that I did not deserve, but then you came back demanding I pretend none of that ever happened."

"I said I was sorry," she whines. "How long are you going to hold this over my head?"

"I'm done now. We're done. Forever. And I won't be giving you a single thing for my dog. Don't ever come near me or Tank again. I plan to press charges against you for stealing—"

"He's mine!" she protests.

"And for breaking and entering."

She crosses her arms and pouts. "The laundry room window was unlocked."

Eli adds some of his cop authority. "Still breaking and entering, even if you didn't break a window to get in."

She glares at him.

I continue. "If you sign something acknowledging Tank's mine, I'll drop the charges. Though I'll still file a restraining order against you. I don't want you anywhere near me ever again."

She bursts into tears. "It's not fair. I have nothing."

"Then you have everything to gain," I say evenly.

Eli lifts a brow at me with a small smirk.

Amelia gestures toward Tank. "At least give me something for him. He's worth four thousand dollars."

"I give you a get-out-of-jail-free card by not pressing charges."

Peter walks into the room holding a small notepad that he shoves at Amelia. "Here. Write it out and give him back the dog. Really, Amelia, I don't know what's wrong with you lately."

She sniffles and scribbles a note. Peter hands it to me and wipes his hands in the air like the business is finished and then walks off.

I read the note over. She did what I asked. Tank's all mine.

"I missed him," Amelia says in a small voice. "I missed us."

"Thank you," I say.

And then I hoist Tank into my arms and carry him out to the car with a big smile on my face. He snuffles and rests his head on my shoulder. One door closed permanently. Now to figure out how to keep another door open.

16

The next day I'm working on built-in shelves in a mansion in a wealthy town about a half hour from Summerdale. I filled Kayla in on the Amelia incident early this morning and let her know Amelia's permanently out of my life. We didn't get to talk long, though, because Kayla was on her way to another meeting at Noon Pharmaceuticals. It's now afternoon, and time seems to have slowed down as I wait to hear how her meeting went.

My phone vibrates, and I take it from my jeans' pocket. My stomach drops at the text.

Kayla: *I got the job!!! Incredible starting salary, benefits, and they'll cover the cost of the move.*

I swallow hard and text back. *Congratulations!*

Kayla: *I didn't tell them yes. I told them I need to think about it and check in with the other companies I interviewed at.*

Relief washes through me. I hadn't even thought of that. She's smart, looking for more offers so she can weigh all her options.

Me: *Keep me posted.*

Kayla: *I will. I miss you. I'll be home Friday night. It's good I stayed to visit Livvie because the VP guy wants me to tour more of their facilities and also invited me to a dinner with more VIPs.*

They really want her. I want her too, but what do I have to

offer her? Sure, I own my own house, and she likes Summerdale, but it can't compare to a flying start at a new career.

Me: *You'll do great.*

Kayla: *Thanks. I love you. And I can't wait to see you again.*

Warmth spreads through my chest. She's so affectionate, so open and loving.

Me: *Love you too.*

I put the phone away and let out a long breath. This is my fault. If I hadn't been so careful to keep my distance, we could've been making plans *here*. She might not even have bothered interviewing far away.

Now the offer is on the table, and she has something real to lose by being with me.

~

Kayla

I am living the dream! I'm madly in love, finally know what great sex is about, and my career is about to begin. Wyatt advised me on how best to use my offer to get counteroffers, and now I've got another offer in Boston, one in New Jersey, not far from where I grew up, and an invitation to meet with a Manhattan company for a third time, which probably means an offer. It's nice to be wanted.

I just got home a short time ago. I showered right away, and then I put on my first lingerie ever. A silver satin and lace slip that's sheer on top and part of the back. Livvie and I went shopping for it. She met Adam when we all went out for dinner and drinks, and she's thrilled for me. I also got an assortment of cute camis and shorts sets, as well as sexy bra and panty sets in silk, satin, and lace. It was a splurge, but I'll have a decent paycheck soon. And I finally have someone to show it off for.

I throw my red dress over the slip, put on black heels, grab my purse, and head out. Time to seduce my man. It was hard to be away from him this week, though I admit I was sore after our weekend together. Probably shouldn't have had so much sex, but I kept insisting I was fine because I was making up for lost time.

I make the short drive to his house and ring the bell. Tank makes a halfhearted bark through the window. *Oof.* I wave at him. I wasn't at all surprised Amelia pulled a sneaky dognapping move like that. The thought had crossed my mind when I was putting the GPS tracker on his collar. She's a little off. Thankfully, she's completely out of the picture. Adam told me he ran into her dad a few days ago, who said she moved in with a friend in Queens. Too bad it isn't as far away as California, but it sounds like she's given up on my man.

Adam answers a moment later.

I beam. "Hi, lover!"

His dark eyes smolder into mine as he pulls me inside. My breath hitches. I know that lusty look.

He shuts the door behind me and pins me against it, his mouth crashing over mine. *He missed me.* His hard body presses against mine, and then he's lifting me, grinding against me as he kisses me again and again.

"Missed you." *Deep kiss.* "Kayla." His mouth leaves a hot trail down my neck. "Love."

"I have something to show you."

He sets me back on my feet, dipping his head to suck on my neck as his hand slides under my dress. "Later."

"It's for you." My breath catches as his fingers slide under my panties. He strokes me, his mouth returning to mine, consuming me. My knees weaken, my fingers tangling in his shirt. One finger eases inside me and then another, his thumb rubbing small circles on pleasure central. Everything narrows down to that one spot of sparking fiery need. I clutch his shirt as my limbs weaken.

He dips his head, whispering urgently in my ear, "Come for me, Kayla. I need it. I need to feel you break."

The intensity instantly ratchets up, his fingers working magic, taking me higher. I break violently, shuddering against him. He murmurs praise by my ear. I lean back against the wall, trying to catch my breath, too spent to even lift a hand.

I hear a zipper, a rustling sound, and then he's lifting me.

My eyes fly open as he lines us up and slowly slides inside me. He was fast with the condom, even faster to join with me. I pant, shocked at this new sensation, taking him from this position. He kisses a hot trail along my neck, murmuring in my ear, "So tight. Relax. I got you."

He lowers me onto him, opening me, filling me. My body strains to accommodate him. I moan softly, and his mouth covers mine, kissing me deeply, stealing my breath, my thoughts, as he finally takes me to the hilt. And then he's thrusting into me, his momentum carrying us both along on an intense ride. I cling to his shoulders as sensations overwhelm me—coiling, hot need, deep pressure, his big hands gripping my hips.

My body tightens around him, my release close, so close. His mouth covers mine, swallowing my soft cries as my body shudders against him in harsh jerks.

"Yes," he says fiercely by my ear, pumping deep once more. I gasp, and he rocks against me as his own release hits. He holds me tight, breathing hard.

A long moment later, he lifts me off him and wraps his arms around me. I rest my head weakly against his chest. I realize suddenly that he gets off watching me get off. He said he needed to feel me break. Everything that happened between us before wasn't as one-sided as I feared. My pleasure was his pleasure too.

I lift my head and smile. "I think I need to lie down. My legs are sort of wobbly."

He steps back and adjusts his jeans, zipping and buttoning. "I couldn't wait. I'll go slower next time, make it better for you."

I laugh a little. "That was plenty good."

He scoops me up, cradled in his arms, and carries me upstairs. I spot Tank curled up on the sofa, sound asleep. "Guess we just looked like animals doing their thing to Tank."

"He's tired out because I made him take his walk."

I play with the hair at the nape of his neck. "Guess I didn't need the lingerie to seduce you."

"Only need you. What kind of lingerie?"

"You'll see. That was an interesting position. It felt like I was riding a giant pole."

He sets me down in the hallway and grins. "A giant pole, huh? I like the comparison."

"It was hard to take you at first, but then it was really deep and good."

He pins me against the wall and kisses me, his fingers tangling in my hair. When he finally lets me up for air, he murmurs, "Sweetest dirty talker I ever heard."

This pleases me. I had no idea I knew how to dirty talk.

He takes my hand and guides me to his room. It's my first time seeing it. The furniture is gorgeous, I'm sure made by hand. A king-size bed with a light wood curved headboard, matching nightstands, and a dresser with elegant curved lines and scrolled legs. The comforter is royal blue, standing out against all the light wood.

"I love your room," I say.

"Show me your lingerie."

I pull my dress off, take the time to set it neatly on the dresser, and turn back to him. "Do you like it?"

His gaze smolders. "You're so beautiful, Kayla. I can't believe I waited so long for this."

I rush into his arms. "We have it now. That's all that matters."

He cups my jaw, his finger stroking along my neck. "I don't want you to leave Summerdale, but I can't ask you to stay."

"You wouldn't move for me?"

"I love where I live. All my clients are here, my family too. I'd have to start my business from scratch somewhere else."

"I love it here too." I consider us and my future prospects, and it's just not clear to me at all. "I think we need to be practical and table that discussion until we know all of our options. Worst case, we can visit each other."

He frowns.

"Please. Let's not talk about the future until we have all the facts. I still have one more interview before I make a decision. I feel so good right now here with you. Come to bed and cuddle me."

"I'm not a cuddler," he grumbles. "Give me a few minutes."

I nod.

He goes to his en suite bathroom.

I flop back on his bed. Oh, it's so comfortable. I get under the covers and wait. Then I turn on my side to make it easier for him to spoon me.

I hear the bathroom door open. "Ready for my spooning."

He slides under the covers and spoons me from behind. "I'm telling you right now this spooning won't last long."

"Why don't you like cuddling?"

He rocks his hips against me. "You turn me on too much."

My lips curl up. "How did you resist me for so long, then?"

"Many showers."

"No wonder you always smelled so fresh and clean."

He whispers in my ear, "I imagined your plump lips around me, fucking me with your mouth."

I turn in his arms. "Let's do that in the shower. I want to make all your fantasies come true."

He groans and turns me back, his hand sliding from my stomach up to cup my breast. "I've got a helluva lot I want to show you. I hope you can spend the whole weekend."

My breath hitches as he caresses my breast, my nipple tightening. "I took off the weekend so I could rest up after my trip. I'm ready for the Adam sex tutorial."

He bites my neck, and my breath shudders out. "You won't be getting much rest."

17

Adam

After an extraordinary weekend together, the following week went by faster than I'd like. Isn't that always the way when you're dreading something? Kayla has to give her answer to her multiple job offers on Monday. Today, Friday, is her final interview in Manhattan. She's an impressive candidate. Brilliant, multiple research papers to her credit, enthusiastic, and a team player. I'm sure they see her as a good long-term investment.

I'm meeting her at a nice restaurant in the city for dinner for one important reason—I'm taking myself out of the equation. She can choose whatever job she believes suits her best without a single worry about me.

That's how much I love her.

≈

Kayla

If I could whistle, I'd totally be whistling a jaunty tune as I walk to the seafood restaurant in Manhattan to meet my dreamy boyfriend for our date. My interview today ended with an on-the-spot offer. I'm excited, but I want to sleep on it before giving an answer to all of my job offers. I have four now to consider. I crunched the numbers immediately after, and when you consider salary, the various benefits, and cost of living in the different areas, they're all roughly equivalent. It really comes down to where I'll feel most comfortable.

I spot Adam standing on the sidewalk outside the restaurant, wearing a dark gray suit with a tie too. He got a haircut, though he still has the light scruff on his jaw that I love.

"Adam!" I practically run into his arms, as well as I can in my pumps. I'm still in my smart light blue interview suit—blazer, silk shell, skirt, and pumps.

He hugs me and pulls back, looking serious. "How'd it go?"

"They made me a sweet offer."

He smiles, shaking his head. "I knew it. You're a dream candidate."

I blush. "You're biased. I'm sure I'm not everyone's dream candidate."

"Four offers."

I grin. "There is that."

He opens the glass door for me, and we head inside the restaurant. It's two levels of seating with cool glass sculptures hanging from the ceiling that look like sea plants, seahorses, and fish. Sconces on the wall provide soft romantic lighting. The tables are dark glossy wood, along with the hardwood floors, the walls a pale aqua.

Adam gives his name to the guy at the front desk, and we're taken up to the top level to a back room with a window view. It's still light outside, so we can see the city clearly, all the hustle and bustle of people and cars.

The host pulls out my seat for me at a corner table for two. I sit down. "Thank you."

He hands me a drink menu. "You're welcome. Enjoy."

After he leaves, I lean across the table to Adam. "It's so nice. How did you hear about this place?"

His eyes shift toward the archway leading to the other room. "I looked it up online."

I scan the drink menu. "I feel like getting something special to drink."

"How about champagne?"

I beam. "Would you drink some with me?"

"Absolutely."

I put the menu down. "Great. So how was your day?"

"Good." He glances toward the other room again.

"Are you looking for the waiter?"

"Yeah."

"You must really be hungry."

He studies me. "How are you? Are you tense from a long afternoon of interviews?"

"Not at all. It was fun. There's no pressure when I know I already have job offers in my pocket."

He takes off his blazer, hanging it on the back of his chair, and tugs at his tie. "Do you want to take off your blazer?"

"Sure." I take it off mostly because I think he wants to see more of me. I'm wearing a white sleeveless silk shell under it. His gaze tracks from my bare shoulder to my arm back up to my exposed collarbone, my neck, and finally my mouth. Lust rushes through my veins. The man can do that with only a look.

He lets out a breath; then he wipes his brow. He's sweating.

"You look like you're overheated. Were you walking around the city in your suit for a while this afternoon?" It's July. That would overheat anyone.

"No, I—there he is."

The waiter arrives with two glasses of champagne, smiling at us. "As requested." That's strange. We didn't order yet.

"Thanks," Adam says tersely.

I smile at the waiter and turn to Adam, confused. "How did he know?"

The waiter disappears just as quickly as he arrived.

Adam takes a deep breath. "Kayla, I know you have so many great opportunities ahead of you, and I never want to be the person who holds you back. You won't need to give me a second thought. I'm taking myself out of the equation."

I blink a few times, confused. It sounds like he's breaking

up with me, yet he ordered us champagne like it's a celebration. "What are you saying?"

He shakes his head, frowning. "I'm messing this up. I love you."

"I love you too," I say slowly.

"And I never want to hold you back. You're brilliant, and I know you're going to do great things in your future."

My heart thumps harder. *Why is he breaking up with me with champagne? What kind of sick gesture is this?* "Adam—"

"Will you marry me?"

I clap a hand over my mouth.

He opens his palm, where apparently he's been holding a diamond engagement ring for a while now. There's a mark on his palm from it. I stare at the ring, a gold band with a marquise-cut diamond.

And then he's on one knee by my side. "I'll go with you wherever you want. I'm in this forever, and I want you to know that before you have to make a big decision. I'm not the one holding you back. I'm the one who's got your back."

I burst into tears and throw my arms around his neck. "Adam! Yes! Omigod, I can't believe you did this romantic gesture."

He slides the ring on my finger and gives me a watery smile. "I can be romantic. I mean it, Kayla. We're together no matter what, anywhere in the world."

I grab his head and kiss him. "I love you so much."

He stands and pulls me into his arms. "I love you too."

Applause breaks out from the tables around us. The waiter who served us champagne walks over to our table, smiling. "Would you like me to take your picture?"

Adam hands over his phone and puts his arms around me from behind. I hold up my ring hand and beam.

The waiter returns the phone, and Adam and I take our seats, accepting congratulations from nearby diners.

I clink my champagne glass against his and take a sip. "Well, that was exciting. For a minute there, I thought you were breaking up with me."

He shakes his head. "No way. I was sweating it out, worried you wouldn't say yes."

"Of course I said yes! I love you."

He lowers his voice. "The first time I asked, you turned me down. Back in Indianapolis."

"That's because you didn't say you loved me. Now I know you do." I smile at my sparkly ring, feeling only pure happiness. Not one single doubt. Not even a worry that he'll leave me at the altar, which I thought would haunt me forever. Adam is a man you can trust to follow through.

And then I know exactly how I want my future to go.

I smile at him. "I have good news. The offer I got today was for the research branch of their company, which is in the suburbs, about a half-hour commute from Summerdale. I'm going to tell them yes."

He gets serious, taking my hand. "I only want you to take it if you'll be happy there. Not because of me."

"I love the work they're doing, I love you, and I love Summerdale. And if that's not reason enough, I also want to be close to Wyatt and Sydney. They'll probably have kids in a couple of years, and I want to be part of that. And vice versa, I want them to be part of our kids' lives. You see, it's a decision that takes into account all aspects of how I want my future to look. I feel great about it."

He kisses the back of my hand. "You are an *incredible* woman. I'm so lucky you're marrying me."

I lean forward and whisper, "You didn't look so lucky when I first asked you to take my virginity. More like alarmed."

He leans across the table and kisses me. "You're a force of nature. I didn't stand a chance."

EPILOGUE

Kayla

It's the end of summer, and I'm enjoying my first moonlight regatta on Lake Summerdale. Adam and I are in his rowboat with Tank, who's wearing a life vest. He can swim with it, but it's tough for him without. It's basically a party on the lake. Tons of people are floating by with glow sticks, LED lights, and lanterns.

We have a camping lantern and matching glow-stick necklaces, which Jenna gave out to everyone. Drew used rope to tie our boats together in one big floating mass. Jenna and Audrey are in a canoe together, Wyatt and Sydney are on a Sunfish sailboat without the dogs since there's no room for them. They have a rowboat they take Snowball and Rexie out in sometimes. Drew and Caleb are in a canoe, my future brothers-in-law. Eli is on cop duty. A few of our friends from the restaurant are here too, the bartender Betsy and the chef Spencer are in a boat with the host guy Sam and another waitress.

I search the sky. It's not quite a full moon but close enough. "Isn't this romantic?"

"It is when you're newly engaged," Sydney answers.

Adam splashes her. "I can answer my fiancée for myself. Yes, Kayla, it's romantic."

"I told you guys how he proposed, right?" I ask, checking in with Sydney, Jenna, and Audrey. Of course I did, the very next day. "That was super romantic too."

"Glad Adam's got his head on straight," Wyatt barks. "Else I would've had to kill him."

"Wyatt!" I exclaim.

"What?"

I shake my head at him. He needs to stop being so over-protective of me. I'm not a kid anymore. "Can you just be happy for us?"

He gestures to Adam. "I like the guy. I just told him to take you seriously, which he did. Good job, Adam."

Adam lifts his brows. "I have so many things I'd like to say to that, but let's keep this civil."

Wyatt smirks. "Come at me."

"Wyatt!" Sydney exclaims. "The boat will tip, and I'm not taking a dive in the water. You guys can wrestle when we get back to shore."

Wyatt points at his eyes and then points to Adam.

I smile at Adam, who's doing beautifully ignoring my brother. "You look very handsome in your shirt."

He looks down at it. "How many occasions do I need to wear it?" It's a black T shirt that says Groom. I'm wearing a matching one that says Bride.

I squint for a moment, thinking. "Let's see, every romantic occasion, of which I'm sure there'll be many. Our engagement party at my mom's house next weekend, rehearsal dinner, definitely on the honeymoon." We're getting married next June and living together in the meantime. I wanted time to plan a beautiful wedding. I helped Sydney plan hers and really got into it. Mine will be at this old estate I found nearby that's used for formal functions. Our honeymoon will be in Hawaii, which I've always wanted to visit. Adam's never been there either.

I hear some snickering and turn to glare at my future brothers-in-law Drew and Caleb. They're pulling at their shirts, doing some kind of mocking sashay action over there, making fun of Adam's groom shirt. "I can only hope one day you guys have a loving bride who gives you romantic gifts too."

"I can only hope," Caleb says with a straight face.

Drew busies himself getting another beer from the cooler, but I don't miss his smirk.

"Force of nature," Adam murmurs, leaning forward to kiss me. "I love that you care about stuff like our shirts."

"Thank you. It's nice to be appreciated." I turn on our waterproof speaker to play some cheerful party music for everyone.

"Turn it up," Wyatt calls.

I do, and he starts dancing in place, making Sydney laugh, who shakes her shoulders toward him. Everyone starts dancing in place, rocking their heads and shimmying. Except for Drew. He's kind of a straight arrow. But he watches Audrey, who's doing this funny head swing, making her long black hair fly all around. I believe he's secretly in love with her, but holds back for some reason. Maybe he doesn't know he's in love. I told Adam about my theory, and he said to stay out of it because Drew wouldn't respond well to being informed he's in love. But Drew's never been in love, so how would he know? I really want to give him a clue, but I respect the boundary Adam set.

A firework goes off in the distance, whistling through the air. Tank barks his *oof* sound, looking toward me for comfort. I shift to put an arm around his trembling shoulders. "It's okay, just noise. Look how pretty."

He leans against my leg. He's scared of the oddest things. Adam says it's because Tank's not so smart. If you open a pizza box, he freaks because he thinks it's giant jaws opening. Other dogs make him nervous too, but then he warms up. And thunder spooks him, and I guess fireworks too.

Adam shifts to sit next to me on the bench, wrapping an arm around me. We watch the fireworks display on the opposite shore with starbursts of yellow, red, and purple. I sigh happily. This is the perfect life for me. A lakeside community, family and friends close by, a fiancé I'm crazy about, and a cool job. It's only been a month at my new job, but I'm very happy there. My boss is amazing. We get along so well. She says I remind her a lot of herself just starting out there.

After the fireworks, everyone packs up to go, rowing back to shore.

I linger behind on the shore, talking to Wyatt and Sydney while Adam puts the rowboat back on a trailer he hooked to the back of his car. I share the latest details I've firmed up for next weekend's engagement party at my mom's house. It's an ocean theme with the idea that there's two less fish in the sea now. (One day we'll go fishing on the ocean at a reasonable hour, and I'll be sure to pack a delicious lunch.) I'm setting up a photo station for our party, planning a ring hunt for plastic jeweled rings with a prize, and taking wedding song requests for our future playlist.

"And the rest is a surprise." I don't want to give away all the fun stuff I have planned.

"Cool," Sydney says. "You're so cute with those Bride and Groom T-shirts."

Wyatt grimaces. "Adam is so whipped."

Sydney elbows him in the ribs. "Watch it. That's my brother."

"And that's my girly sister," he says, gesturing toward me. "I'm glad he's whipped. Less chance he'll end up hurting her."

"Oh, he'd never hurt me," I say confidently. "Adam's a great guy."

Sydney smiles over my shoulder a split second before I'm lifted in the air and swung around.

Adam sets me down, holds my face in his hands, and kisses me. "I heard you singing my praises."

"Of course. I always do."

He grins and looks over at Sydney. "She'll show anyone my portfolio of work. Complete strangers."

"He's an artist with wood," I say.

Wyatt snickers.

I glare at him and then turn to Adam for backup. He's biting back a smile. "What?"

"Nothing. Let's go home."

"I love the sound of that. Home."

We say goodbye and walk hand in hand back to where he parked the car across the way at The Horseman Inn. A lot of people parked there and along the road behind it, as instructed to. It was all marked off by Eli and his boss, Chief Daniels. The police chief is in his late sixties and planning to retire, which means Eli will get a promotion soon.

I spot Eli, out of uniform, talking with big animated gestures to someone in a red Honda Accord. Jenna has that car, but it could be someone else. Eli must've joined us late to watch the fireworks after his shift. As we get closer, I realize he's gesturing angrily.

"Uh-oh," Adam says. "I think someone backed into Eli's car."

The person steps out of their car, and I recognize tall blond Jenna. She walks around to examine the back of her car.

It looks like she backed into Eli's brand-new shiny silver Mustang. He showed it off to Adam when he bought it. I dutifully admired it too.

"Calm down," Jenna says. "It's a little ding. I'm sure they can fix it."

"Did you even look before you backed up?" Eli shouts.

"I have a backup camera," she says. "It just wasn't working for a moment because I pressed the radio."

Eli stalks closer to her, his voice dropping too low to make out the words.

She looks up at him and licks her lips, her shoulders pulling back. It almost looks flirtatious. She shifts away suddenly. "I'll pay for it, okay? Just let me know how much." She gets in her car and drives away.

Eli runs a hand through his hair, watching her before turning back to his car.

Adam speaks up. "That sucks. You've had it, what, two weeks?"

"Yeah," Eli says, looking a little dazed.

"Sorry, man," Adam says, heading for his car.

I follow Adam, and as soon as we're in the privacy of our car, Tank in the back seat with the windows down, I share my latest keen observation. "I think Jenna's going to hook up with Eli."

His head whips toward mine. "No way. She just ruined his new car."

"It's not ruined just dinged, and now they have a reason to talk. I read the body language on Jenna. I've seen her flirt with the delivery guy. And Eli seemed dazed."

He holds me by the chin and kisses me. "You, my brilliant little matchmaker, have got to stop seeing love everywhere just because we're swimming in it."

"Do you think it would be difficult to make love in the lake?"

He chuckles, starts the car, and heads toward home. "What in the world made you think of that?"

"Swimming in love."

"It's doable if you're not in too deep. But we're not doing that because the lake's public and surrounded by houses."

"Remember our picnic in that shady spot by the lake on one of our first dates? That was pretty private over there." *Until his ex showed up.* I never mention her name. She doesn't exist as far as I'm concerned.

He glances over at me. "Would the shower work?"

"Yes. And we'll try the water in Hawaii on our honeymoon. We won't know anyone there and can do it under the moonlight. I'm glad I went on the pill so we can be spontaneous like that. By the way, I'm getting us matching swimsuits and, of course, bride and groom baseball caps to wear on the beach. That way everyone will know we're newlyweds. They'll probably all be extra nice to us and pile on perks like free drinks and extra flower leis."

"Love your enthusiasm. That's all I can say."

I squeeze his arm. His ex-fiancée wasn't enthusiastic about any part of their engagement. He didn't realize how much that bothered him until I went full steam ahead with all my excitement over our wedding and honeymoon. We're waiting on kids for a few years. I've got time and want to enjoy just the two of us. And Tank of course.

Once we're back home again, we get Tank taken care of,

and get ready for bed. I love that I get to cuddle with Adam every night. He's *so* good at it.

I turn off the light on the nightstand, slide into bed next to him, and roll to my side so he can spoon me. His knees tuck under mine, his arm banding around my waist.

The heat of his body warms my bare back. We made an agreement. He'll spoon me every night as long as we're naked.

His hand roams, as it always does, coasting over my skin, caressing my breasts, sliding between my legs. Sparks fire everywhere he touches, a languid heat taking over my limbs. He kisses a hot trail along my neck, his fingers gently stroking me in tantalizing circles. I melt into him, letting him take me on a slow journey of pleasure. He's much more aggressive and demanding in daylight hours. At night, it's slow and easy. I love it every way.

Pleasure builds and builds, my breath coming harder. He's in tune to every movement I make, every sound, every breath. Giving me more when I need it, slowing it down when I'm close, but always, always pushing me to greater heights. I cry out as my hips jerk, my climax roaring through me.

He immediately hitches my thigh up and enters me, pushing as deep as he can go. I moan. He rocks into me, seeking just the right movement until I gasp. He keeps going, right there, right where I need him, his fingers trailing down to my sex, stroking me gently. I grab his wrist, the intensity almost too much. I don't know if I'm trying to keep him there or push him away. My back arches, and I grab his shoulder from behind me, my nails digging in.

He murmurs in my ear, dirty words of encouragement, urging me on, telling me he's going to take good care of me. I'm wild with need, rocking back into him, my body tight and hot. Oh God.

I'm chanting his name, trembling as he rocks into me, his fingers relentless. I break with a harsh cry, my body clenching around him, even as he pushes me open, over and over. I'm coming in wave after wave of endless pleasure. He pumps deep again and again until his own release takes hold, his hand clamping onto my hip, holding me tight to him.

I'm still catching my breath when he rolls me to my back and kisses me soundly on the mouth. I reach up and stroke his hair, too spent to speak.

His words run hot over my lips. "I told you I'm not much of a cuddler."

My lips curl up. "Your version of cuddling totally works for me."

"I love you so damn much."

My heart squeezes. "I knew from the start. You were the guy. Nobody else came close."

He pulls me into his arms, so we're facing each other side by side. He kisses my forehead, my nose, my lips. "Love. Sleep."

He speaks in monosyllables sometimes, but I get the message. He loves me fiercely. And I wore him out.

I close my eyes and let out a soft sigh. He's a secret cuddler afterward. I won't mention it. I like the way he proves he's not a cuddler every night.

My Adam. Cuddler, craftsman extraordinaire, and my best sexiest friend.

Don't miss the next book in the series, *Sporting*, where Eli and Jenna take an unexpected road trip together!

Sporting

Jenna

After accidentally dinging a brand-new car, I'm suddenly face-to-face with an angry alpha male. And the sparks are flying.

Wait. Eli Robinson?

How's it possible the irritating younger brother of my best friend has morphed into this gorgeous swaggering man?

I can't let myself be tempted. Eli is off-limits. My best friend, his sister who helped raise him, makes sure I know it.

Except the more I get to know him, the more difficult it is to stay away. This can only end badly. No relationship is worth losing my best friend.

And then he kidnaps me.

Eli

Once upon a time, Jenna Larsen was my teenaged dream girl, and I mean that in the dirtiest way possible. Now that we're adults, I discovered she's even better than I dreamed. We can't keep our hands off each other. But I want more. So I took her on a surprise getaway to move things beyond the bedroom. An extended date of sorts. Fine. I kidnapped her. We needed to get away from judging eyes.

I only hope she stops being mad long enough to give us a chance.

Sign up for my newsletter and never miss a new release! kyliegilmore.com/newsletter

ALSO BY KYLIE GILMORE

Unleashed Romance <<steamy romcoms with dogs!

Fetching (Book 1)

Dashing (Book 2)

Sporting (Book 3)

Toying (Book 4)

Blazing (Book 5)

Happy Endings Book Club Series <<the Campbell family and a romance book club collide!

Hidden Hollywood (Book 1)

Inviting Trouble (Book 2)

So Revealing (Book 3)

Formal Arrangement (Book 4)

Bad Boy Done Wrong (Book 5)

Mess With Me (Book 6)

Resisting Fate (Book 7)

Chance of Romance (Book 8)

Wicked Flirt (Book 9)

An Inconvenient Plan (Book 10)

A Happy Endings Wedding (Book 11)

The Clover Park Series <<brothers who put family first!

The Opposite of Wild (Book 1)

Daisy Does It All (Book 2)

Bad Taste in Men (Book 3)

Kissing Santa (Book 4)

Restless Harmony (Book 5)

Not My Romeo (Book 6)

Rev Me Up (Book 7)

An Ambitious Engagement (Book 8)

Clutch Player (Book 9)

A Tempting Friendship (Book 10)

Clover Park Bride: Nico and Lily's Wedding

A Valentine's Day Gift (Book 11)

Maggie Meets Her Match (Book 12)

The Clover Park STUDS series <<hawt geeks who unleash into studs!

Almost Over It (Book 1)

Almost Married (Book 2)

Almost Fate (Book 3)

Almost in Love (Book 4)

Almost Romance (Book 5)

Almost Hitched (Book 6)

The Rourkes Series <<swoonworthy princes and kickass princesses!

Royal Catch (Book 1)

Royal Hottie (Book 2)

Royal Darling (Book 3)

Royal Charmer (Book 4)

Royal Player (Book 5)

Royal Shark (Book 6)

Rogue Prince (Book 7)

Rogue Gentleman (Book 8)

Rogue Rascal (Book 9)

Rogue Angel (Book 10)

Rogue Devil (Book 11)

Rogue Beast (Book 12)

Check out my website for the most up-to-date list of my books: kyliegilmore.com/books

ABOUT THE AUTHOR

Kylie Gilmore is the *USA Today* bestselling author of the Unleashed Romance series, the Rourkes series, the Happy Endings Book Club series, the Clover Park series, and the Clover Park STUDS series. She writes humorous romance that makes you laugh, cry, and reach for a cold glass of water.

Kylie lives in New York with her family, two cats, and a nutso dog. When she's not writing, reading hot romance, or dutifully taking notes at writing conferences, you can find her flexing her muscles all the way to the high cabinet for her secret chocolate stash.

Sign up for Kylie's Newsletter and get a FREE book! kyliegilmore.com/newsletter

For text alerts on Kylie's new releases, text KYLIE to the number 21000. (US only)

For more fun stuff check out Kylie's website https://www.kyliegilmore.com.

Thanks for reading *Dashing*. I hope you enjoyed it. Would you like to know about new releases? You can sign up for my new release email list at kyliegilmore.com/newsletter. I promise not to clog your inbox! Only new release info, sales, and some fun giveaways.

I love to hear from readers! You can find me at:
kyliegilmore.com
Instagram.com/kyliegilmore
Facebook.com/KylieGilmoreToo
Twitter @KylieGilmoreToo

If you liked Adam and Kayla's story, please leave a review on your favorite retailer's website or Goodreads. Thank you.

Manufactured by Amazon.ca
Bolton, ON

31391871R00103